Death Comes to the Rector

David Q. Hall

Volume One in the *Death Most Unholy* Series

Printed in the United States of America
First Printing 2017
ISBN 13: 978-0692889794
ISBN10: 0692889795

Tree Shadow Press

www.treeshadowpress.com

Cover art by Matt McCormick.

WHAT READERS ARE SAYING:

Lust, rejection and envy make a caustic combination in David Quincy Hall's first novel. There is Big Tiny, a shred of ancient papyrus, an old college girlfriend – recently widowed – who is hiding a dark, dark life. This story twists and turns, and just when the mystery seems solved, a blindsiding blow. Written as only an insider of the clergy could know, the surprises will at times steal your breath away.
~ *Richard Alan Hall, author of the best-selling Big Bay Series of Novels Traverse City, Michigan*

An Angel of Death visits a rector in Pennsylvania, producing a mystery that leads to the far reaches of Northwest Michigan. Pastor and first-time novelist David Hall brings his background with guns and the Episcopalians to produce a gripping page turner, an all-together good read!
~ *Brad Spencer, Award-winning teacher of writing and journalism, freelance writer and columnist*

Dave Hall takes us into the bizarre life of an unknown, heartless killer. At the same time, also into the world of the all-too-human pastors and their church families. As I wove in and out of one mystery after another, I found that I couldn't put this book down. Each page brought new details, twists and intrigue. I wanted more!
~ *Margaret Myers, The Presbyterian Church of Traverse City, Michigan*

I enjoyed David's novel very much – an exciting plot with great characters set in a beautiful spot in northern Michigan....Leelanau County. I look forward to his next work, hopefully keeping many of the same unique, colorful characters.
~ *Scott Gemmell, champion shotgunner*

Pastor, sportsman and traveler David Q. Hall writes about what he knows in his debut novel, *Death Comes to the Rector*. David's ability to share familiar details of place, people, actions and customs draws you into every nuance of the story. As you read, you feel you know the people and places and as a result you are not merely a reader, but a witness. This classic who-done-it has twists and turns that will keep you reading long after you should turn out the light.
~ *Steve Wade, Episcopal Church*

DEDICATION

This Book is dedicated to my beloved wife, Maxine, our daughters, Lisa and Rebekah, our son-in-law, Doug, and grandson Stephan. Their love and support make writing a joy as well as a journey.

They thought I could do it.

ACKNOWLEDGMENTS

Richard Alan Hall and Debra Hall, Jill Beauchamp, Brad Spencer, Margie Myers, Scott Gemmel, Steve Wade, Joe Charlevoix, and a host of others, including numerous good church people, seemed to agree that of course a retired pastor could write murder mysteries.

Matt McCormick contributed his talent by designing and illustrating the covers.

I thank them for their help in numerous respects.

Thank you also to Tree Shadow Press for taking me on as an author.

CHAPTER ONE

The Church of the Resurrection, Episcopal, had long been one of the best-known and most beautiful of the dark-stone churches of Pittsburgh. Occupying an entire block with its buildings and grounds in the prestigious Shadyside area, its membership was heavily comprised of "old money" steel and foundry families. Although some of the old formalities and customs had relaxed in modern times, the curb in front of the main entrance would still be filled with chauffeured Rolls and Mercedes on a Sunday morning.

But it was not wealthy worshipers that approached the church this Easter Sunday morning. Sweeping down the wide front walk, through the high, massive, red doors and through the leaded glass-adorned narthex, came the Angel of Death.

The Angel was no effete representation of a Christmas card artist with over-large bird wings and lacy gown, nor a chubby, winged baby with miniature lyre, nor even the six-winged creatures full of eyes in front and behind of the Revelation of St. John, but as angels truly are: spiritual beings comprised of incomprehensible, indescribable energy and power. Real angels are so terrorizing and overwhelming to any human being made aware of their presence that the Holy Scriptures preceded an angel-human encounter with the words to the puny person, "Do not be afraid."

The Angel of Death swept down the center aisle of The Church of the Resurrection, past the dark, carved walnut pews flanked by larger-than-life-sized carved statues of the apostles standing on large sconces against the walls, interspersed by Medieval-style deep blue and red stained glass windows. The angel continued over the stone steps leading up to the massive granite Communion Table, straight toward the towering mural of the Resurrection adorning the arch and illustrating the given name of the cathedral-like church. It then banked to the side into the sacristy where vestments, candles, communion ware, robes and the like were kept, and finally into the Rector's Study.

The study would put any corporate CEO's personal office to shame. It was lined floor-to-ceiling with finely-crafted walnut bookcases filled with classic works of theology, biblical commentaries, shelves of church history, and the best and most up-to-date books on biblical archeology. One end of the large office held an antique English walnut conference table with ten matching chairs, all sitting on a massive antique Persian rug that ran under the rector's wide, dark oak desk on the opposite end of the study. When sunlight came later that Easter Day of Resurrection, the three tall stained glass windows would cast soft, colored light on the intricate floral pattern of the hand-woven rug, and on the pool of bright red blood that was seeping into the soft wool.

At one side of the spreading blood lay the beloved pastor's shattered head, the back of it blown grotesquely open by a shotgun blast. Widely spattered drops of blood splayed against the stained glass window behind the desk and the nearby paneled wall. So recently had the horrific act occurred that the rector's heart was in its last, fading beat when the Angel of Death reached down and gathered up the exiting soul. Had the angel and the rector's soul possessed corporeality, the taking up might have been described as heavenly arms cradling and lifting a brother's body, tenderly and lovingly. The actuality of it was more like a spiritual essence merging into the vessel of a greater and more powerful spiritual being. And then they were gone into the timelessness of Eternity, swept into the spiritual Kingdom of Heaven.

CHAPTER TWO

Shortly before 6:00 a.m. on Easter Sunday morning, Joe, the head custodian at Church of the Resurrection, began to unlock the doors. He walked down the office hallway toward the Rector's Study. The door was slightly open and light from a desk lamp shone out into the dim hallway. Joe stuck his head in.

"Good morning, Dr. Brand. Happy Easter."

There was no response. Obviously the rector had arrived already, else the study door would not be open, but Joe hadn't seen or heard him anywhere around the church. Joe took a few steps into the big study. He thought he saw something on the rug, poking out from behind the huge desk. Joe stepped a bit closer.

Then he saw the body of Dr. Brand, the great pool of blood darkening the fine floral patterns of the antique rug, and the shotgun lying next to the body, at an angle. He saw the spattered blood on the big stained glass window behind the desk and sprayed on the wall alongside. It was hard to make out Dr. Brand's head, since it seemed blown apart, the back of it missing in a smear of blood, brain matter, and matted hair.

First complete horror seized Joe's mind, followed very quickly by such an overwhelming wave of nausea that he immediately vomited into the waste basket behind the desk. Stunned and almost paralyzed by the scene before him, somehow Joe thought to grab the phone on the desktop. His fingers didn't seem to want to work, and he fumbled with the simple task of punching 911. The 911 operator answered right away.

"911, please state the nature of your emergency."

"Oh my God, the rector has been shot. I think he's dead. Come quick."

"Someone's been shot? Where are you calling from, sir? Can you give me an address?"

"I...he's...here at the church. Oh my God, please come."

"At the church?" asked the operator. "What church, sir? Can you give me an address, please? Are you with him now? Is he breathing?"

"Church. Church of the Resurrection, you know, the big stone church here in Shadyside. Yes, I'm with him, but he's not moving. Oh my God. He's dead. He's dead."

"Emergency vehicles are on their way, sir. Please stay where you are, and don't touch anything. I'll stay on the phone with you."

"Thank you. Oh my God," Joe replied weakly as he slumped into one of the leather club chairs in front of the desk. He buried his head in his trembling hands while still clutching the phone and waited.

In a matter of minutes, police, ambulance, and a fire truck arrived at the church as darkness was about to turn to dawn. Detective Sergeant James Bradley arrived at the scene and took command of the beginning investigation. A perimeter was established with the usual yellow crime scene tape.

From a kitchen window in the Rectory, Sarah Brand looked out at the rapidly developing scene with its official vehicles and flashing lights. She had come down in her morning sweats for an initial cup of coffee before starting to get ready for Easter services and Easter Breakfast. The door bell rang as the alarming activity whirled around the side door of the church and the parking lot.

Detective Sergeant Bradley and a female uniformed officer were at the door as she opened it. After a brief introduction, Jim asked, "Are you Mrs. Brand?"

"Yes, Sergeant. What's going on? Why are there emergency vehicles over at the church?"

"I'm afraid we have some bad news, Mrs. Brand. It appears

as though your husband, Dr. Brand, is dead in his study at the church. He was found by the church custodian just a bit ago. Could you please come over and identify the body? Officer Lopez will wait if you need to dress and accompany you to the church."

Sarah listened with an expression of disbelief and shock, scarcely hearing what she was being told. She wavered, but steadied herself with a hand on the door frame.

"Yes, of course, just give me a moment to throw some clothes on. Oh, it can't be. It can't be Bill. Not Bill. There must be some mistake."

She swayed as though she might collapse. Officer Lopez caught her arm and guided her to a breakfast nook chair until she was able to steady herself. Choking with tears, Sarah rallied and stood up again.

"I'll be with you as soon as I can. Thank you, officer," she gulped.

"Take as much time as you need, Mrs. Brand," said Officer Lopez.

In a matter of minutes, just before 6:30, Sarah was in Bill's study. Sergeant Bradley was waiting for her.

He guided her gently toward the desk, but softly warned her that what she was about to see would be gruesome and horrifying. "You don't have to look until you feel able."

"Please, Sergeant, I need to see him." Shuddering and frankly unsteady, she nonetheless steeled herself. She nodded feebly, "I'm ready."

She identified the body as that of her husband, and immediately turned away, burying her sobbing face in her hands. Again guided by Jim Bradley and Officer Lopez, her knees buckled underneath her as she sank into the same club chair that Joe the custodian had so recently collapsed into.

"Take your time, Mrs. Brand. When you're ready, Officer Lopez will go with you back to your house, if you want. I can see you again there."

Her long hair hung loosely down both sides of her head, her chin drooped as she shook her head weakly. She spoke with a quavering voice.

"No, no. I'll stay here for now. I don't think I can even walk back to the rectory right now. I'll go to the Church Lounge, just down the hall. I need to make some phone calls."

Once in the lounge, the first call she made was to her oldest and most loyal friend, Daniel Henriks, pastor of a Presbyterian church in the next neighborhood to the south. Then she would call her brother and sister.

CHAPTER THREE

Easter Sunday morning found the Rev. Dr. Daniel (Danny) Henriks in his office early. It was not yet 6:00 am, and not even the church custodian had arrived to start opening doors at the South Presbyterian Church of Pittsburgh, PA. But Danny readily admitted that he was obsessive-compulsive about details, and he was walking briskly around the large building checking on all the arrangements and materials for what was traditionally the most important day of worship in the church year.

Banked rows of Easter lilies stood across the front of the chancel steps, curving down toward the outside ends of the front pews. *"Oh, that one would look better if the pot was turned a bit. There,"* Danny commented to himself. *"That's better."*

Not that many of his worshipers would notice, let alone be critical, but it satisfied his perfectionist tendencies. Worship service bulletins stacked in baskets on pedestals at the side doors from the narthex to the sanctuary? Check. Also on either side of the doors opening to the center aisle? Check.

He knew without bothering to look that the brilliant white, recently dry-cleaned, paraments with gold thread embroidery were hanging from the pulpit, the lectern, and draped over the centrally-placed communion table in the chancel. The giant, carved walnut cross in the alcove at the center-back of the chancel had a long, white satin cloth draped over one of its arms, curved down over the front of the cross with its hand-carved *alpha* and *omega*, and back over the other arm. He had seen to all of that on

Good Friday, after the *"Last Words from the Cross"* service. But he looked anyway, and convinced himself that one end of the cloth hung just a tiny bit lower than the other. Hardly anyone would think so, but he couldn't stand the thought that it was uneven. With the aid of a step ladder kept in the side janitor's closet, he adjusted it to be perfect.

Every other detail and arrangement seemed to be just right, so it was time to head back to his office and go over his well-prepared sermon for the umpteenth time. His Associate Pastor, Tim Murphy, would be arriving any minute to lead and preach at the 7:30 "sunrise service." Dan would preach at the 9:30 and 11:00 traditional services. As he returned to his desk, he chuckled to himself about the Presbyterians' use of "sunrise" for that first Easter service. The sun would have risen over a half-hour before, but it was always at 7:30 – year in and year out – with an Easter breakfast from 8:30 to 9:30 in the Fellowship Hall.

All was ready for a typically beautiful Day of Resurrection.

Danny was about a page into his manuscript when his cell phone rang. Could someone be checking on the times for the services that morning? Maybe on the church phone, but who at 6:30 on Easter Sunday on his cell?

"This is Dr. Henriks. Happy Easter, how may I help you?"

"Oh, Daniel," a familiar voice sobbed on the other end. "It's Sarah." There was more sobbing, "Bill is dead. The police say he committed suicide."

The Rev. Dr. William Brand had long been both a distinguished colleague and one of Danny's best friends. He fought through the instantaneous feeling of shock and numbness, and quickly replied, "Oh, Sarah, I'm so sorry. When? Where? Where are you now?"

"I'm at the church. He did it earlier this morning while I was still in bed. He's still in his study here. Police are everywhere. They're investigating and taping off the whole office area. I don't know what to do." She let go with another painful sobbing.

"Sarah, listen, I'll be right there. Just do what the police tell you to do. It'll only be fifteen minutes, tops, before I get there."

"No, no, you have Easter services. I can't ask you..."

"It'll be okay," Dan interrupted gently. "Tim has the first service. I'll be there and get back here by 8:45 for my service. People will cover while I'm out. Just hang on."

"Okay," she answered weakly.

Pulling on a top coat over his best suit, Danny exited his office and strode through the main church office area. In the hall leading to the back parking lot, he ran into Mel the custodian.

"Mel, I just got a phone call from Sarah Brand. Dr. Brand just died. I need to go over to their church right now, but I won't be gone more than a couple of hours."

"What time will you be back, pastor?"

"No later than 8:45. Please tell any anyone who asks where I am, that I'll be back in plenty of time for the first service."

"I'll take care of it," Mel said. "Drive safe, and we'll have everything ready to go by the time you get back."

As he pulled his Jeep Grand Cherokee from its usual "Reserved for the Pastor" parking spot out onto Baum Boulevard, it occurred to Danny that there was nothing typical about this Easter and what he would soon see was definitely not "beautiful."

CHAPTER FOUR

As Danny pulled up to the Church of the Resurrection, the usual scene of cars belonging to church staff and arriving members was overwhelmed by police cars, emergency vehicles, and the coroner's van. He swung through the parking lot and over to the side door that was nearest to the Rector's Study. If the police investigators were already talking suicide, it wasn't officially a "crime scene." Nevertheless, access to the area of the Rector's Study was being restricted until the investigation was considered complete. Just to be covered, Danny reached into his glove compartment, pulled out his Police Chaplain placard, and placed it in the driver's side corner of his windshield. Then he clipped a laminated ID card bearing the same designation to his lapel.

The officer at the door recognized him at once. "Come in, Chaplain. Head straight down the hall. They're in the priest's office." Danny knew the way, of course. Bill had been a colleague for many years, and he had been at Church of the Resurrection numerous times over those years.

Another uniformed patrolman was manning the door to the study, and welcomed Danny in the same way, "Come in, Chaplain. Detective Sergeant Bradley is right over there." Danny was reassured to know that his old friend Jim Bradley was on the scene. Bradley was as good as the Pittsburgh Police Department had. He was a veteran cop and a skilled investigator. If Jim was saying "suicide," you could put it in the bank.

But any good feeling on seeing Jim Bradley was quickly overwhelmed and shoved aside by his next glance at the covered body lying behind the massive desk, the darkening blood stain on the lush rug. Feeling genuinely affected, but professional enough not to show it, Danny strode over to Sergeant Bradley and shook the offered hand. "I'm glad to see you here, Jim. I just can't believe this."

"Good to see you, too, Chaplain. You'll be a help here. There are a lot of badly shaken folks, including a couple of our officers who knew Father Brand from around Shadyside. He was a friend of yours, I understand?"

"Yes, yes. Bill, his wife, Sarah, and I all went to the University of Pittsburgh together. Sarah and I were undergraduates, Bill a grad student." Danny looked around the cluster of police and others, "In fact, she was the one who called me to come over here. She's....?"

"Just down the hall and around the corner. In the Church Lounge. Feel free to go down there. We'll be wrapping up here soon and they'll be taking the body to the Medical Examiner at the morgue."

"Sarah said on the phone that it looks like suicide?"

"Looks that way, yes." Like any competent investigating detective, Sergeant Bradley was not about to say too much prematurely. "Looks like he fortified himself with a lot of scotch first, took off his right shoe and sock, stuck the business end of his own shotgun in his mouth, then used his right big toe to press down on the trigger. Shotgun's still lying on the floor, but we'll pick it up as soon as photos are all taken and have forensics check it out for prints, any trace evidence. But it looks like he did himself in."

"Okay, Jim, thanks for sharing that much. I'll go down to the lounge and see Sarah. Mind if I glance at the shotgun first?"

"Sure. You know well enough not to touch it, but I'll walk you over there. Slip these on first"

He handed Danny a pair of protective "booties" to slip over his shoes. Preliminary call may have been suicide, but until officially pronounced, the scene and any potential evidence to the contrary were not to be contaminated. They stepped around the big desk, and for the first time Danny could see the whole covered body, the distressingly wide blood pool, and the shotgun. And yes, it was Bill's own, pet trap gun. It was all the normally unflappable Rev. Dr. Henriks could do not to reach down and steady himself on the corner of the desk.

Pushing down the mixture of welling grief, lightheadedness, and a bit of nausea, Danny murmured another "Thanks" to Sergeant Bradley. "Call me back if I can be of any help here," he offered as he turned, slipped off the shoe covers at the study door, and proceeded into the hall.

"You got it." said the detective in reply.

CHAPTER FIVE

As Danny had left the study he glimpsed something that had strangely registered in his confused mind as "this is not right," but before he could think about it he was standing in front of a quietly sobbing Sarah. She looked up at him, her face reddened with grief and tears, but no mascara streaks because she had been called over from the Rectory before she had gotten ready for coming to Easter worship.

"Oh, Daniel," she wailed, rising up to throw her arms around him and let loose with a fresh burst of sobbing. "Sit down with me, please." At that the woman deacon who had been sitting next to Sarah on the love seat, with a comforting arm around her, got up quickly and slipped away. "I don't know what I'm going to do. How can he be gone?"

He sat beside her. "I just can't believe it, either, Sarah. I had talked with him in his study just over a week ago, and he seemed fine. More than fine. Excited and buoyant actually. Did something happen during Holy Week? I don't understand how..." The invariably articulate Dr. Henriks' voice broke off softly as words seemed to fail him for once.

"No, no, there was nothing," Sarah gasped for air. "I mean...he worried about how everyone was going to react to his big discovery...I don't know. I just don't know *anything*." She quietly sobbed into the tissues she clutched.

"There, there," he hugged her, "I'm sorry. I shouldn't be asking questions right now. You know how I am," he said.

The Rev. Dr. Henriks was famous among all who knew him as being as compulsive and thorough in questioning things as he was in arranging the details in his personal, professional, and social life. He just had an unrelenting drive to want to know...everything.

He avoided the well-meaning cliché for Sarah that "It's okay." Nothing about this start to Easter Sunday was okay. "Listen, I'll have to head back to my church pretty soon, but I'll call and come to the Rectory this evening if you want. Will that be good?"

"Please," she nodded. "My sister is coming from Brentwood soon. She'll stay with me for awhile. Then, maybe I'll go to their house. I don't know..." Her voice started to trail off and waver again, then it rallied, "See you tonight." Daniel gave her another gentle hug, a little kiss on her cheek, rose up and left the Lounge.

On his way back past the Rector's Study he poked his head in the doorway. "Sergeant Bradley," he called to the detective, who looked up from his notes. "Okay if I stop by the station this coming week to check on what you've found out?"

"You're always welcome in our house, Chaplain. Forensics will examine the gun right away tomorrow. Should be wrapped up pretty quick." Bradley had apparently checked out enough to sound even more confident.

While Danny was in the Lounge the body had been loaded on a gurney and was about to be wheeled out. Somehow, Easter Sunday would go on...but not with Dr. Brand in the pulpit, a fact that was spreading like bizarre wildfire among the continually arriving worshipers. Danny felt a twinge of guilt about rushing by milling, disbelieving, shocked women of wealth in old-fashioned Easter bonnets, expensive, spring-colored dresses and heels and handbags, past their men in suits and shoes that would wipe out a month of his own salary. But words of support and comfort, if any could so serve, would have to come from Bill's staff members at Church of the Resurrection.

Danny could only pray silently that this particular Day of Resurrection would include the very personal resurrection of his old friend Bill into eternal life with his Lord and Savior in the Kingdom of Heaven. But it was time to be the professional again, and he drove resolutely back to South Presbyterian to do his pastoral duties.

CHAPTER SIX

The Easter services at South Presbyterian had, of course, included announcements about the tragic death of the well-known, highly-respected, Rev. Dr. William Brand, with appropriate prayers for his resurrection into eternal life with Christ. No details had been expressed about the circumstances, not even about the place, the gun, nor any "whys" or "hows", just that it was sudden and unexpected, and please pray for his wife, family, and all the church family of their nearby neighbor in the Christian community of faith.

Danny forced himself to place all of his focus and energy on the requirements of the day. The necessity of expressing Easter joy and celebration. Pulling off, as perfectly as humanly possible, the long-planned worship services. The Easter Breakfast event. Greeting and rejoicing with his longtime members, friends, and visitors at South Presbyterian.

Around mid-afternoon, Danny left the church knowing that the custodian would shut off the lights and lock the doors. He headed home to catch his breath mentally, physically and spiritually for a few hours.

Danny lived alone in an attractive, suburban, two-story house in the South Hills of Pittsburgh. It was more house than he really needed for just himself. His late wife had died, entirely too young, almost ten years ago. Since it had been their home, he couldn't seem to bring himself to sell and leave it. Admittedly, it would have been more sensible to have a two-bedroom condo or townhouse with less to care for. No yard work. More security for those times when he travelled and was away from Pittsburgh and South Presbyterian.

He shed his suit coat, finally loosened that infernal, constricting tie, tossed his keys in their particular section of the organizing basket on his writing desk inside the door from the garage, headed for a kitchen cabinet, and poured himself some Crown Royal Black, neat. He had developed a fondness for the smooth-tasting Canadian whiskey from some of his gun club friends. While it was more expensive than more common Canadians, it cost far less than the rare single-malt scotches that his friend Bill always preferred. Besides, that was a fringe benefit of dropping by to see his colleague at opportune times. Bill never hesitated to share his single-malts.

The late-afternoon, spring day had remained warm and pleasant in Southwestern Pennsylvania, so he stepped out on his back patio, sat down in an Adirondack chair, and sipped. Danny never, ever drank to excess, and was especially conservative and cautious when he was going to be driving. But he enjoyed the relaxing comfort the whiskey provided. It seemed to enable him to ponder things.

Sure enough, without even combing back over the early morning tragedy of Bill's shocking death and its details, it hit him! The thing that he had glimpsed by the wall alongside of the door going out of the Rector's Study just popped into his consciousness. It was a finely-twisted, frayed bit of woven cord. It was small, maybe not even an inch, and though faded, the individual threads had once been bright, intertwined red, yellow, green, black, white, probably other colors. At eye-level above it, next to the door, Bill had hung a multi-colored West African weaving that he had collected on one of his many trips overseas, and at a cursory glance it would seem to have been a bit of fine cord that had frayed off of the weaving somehow and fallen onto the floor below, but Danny's eye for details knew that it wasn't. The colors were close, but not quite the same. Amazingly enough, he just happened to know where it had possibly come from. And, it just didn't seem right that it was there in Bill's study.

He felt an immediate urge to drive back there and look at

the faded, frayed bit of cord more closely, but it was soon time to go to the Rectory and see Sarah again under hopefully calmer circumstances. Maybe Monday morning he could get back to the church and look for it.

Then another disquieting thought pushed through. In the immediate shock of viewing poor Bill's body lying there on the rug, his destroyed head in that pool of blood, he hadn't looked at the shotgun any closer than to note that it was, in fact, Bill's own, classic Remington 1100 trap gun. When he thought about it now, the gun wasn't right, either.

It had a choke tube screwed into the muzzle. He knew from years of shooting with Bill that his friend always, never deviating, waited until he was at the shooting range before screwing in his choice of choke tube for a round of trap. More open if he was going to be at the 16-yard station. More closed if longer range. At home, in the gun safe, he stored his shotguns with semi-auto snap caps. The snap cap would have been removed before loading the gun to kill himself, but longtime habit made it seem unlikely that he would have bothered to screw in a choke tube. What would have been the point?

Danny sipped and wondered.

CHAPTER SEVEN

Driving back up to Shadyside to see Sarah that evening, Danny continued to stew over these little inconsistencies. What was the odd little piece of twisted cord on the floor of the study? Why would a choke tube be screwed in the muzzle of the shotgun? And most of all, why would Bill want to kill himself in the first place? He had seen no signs that Bill was at all depressed. In fact, quite the contrary, the esteemed Dr. Brand had been ecstatic when Danny had visited him in his study the Wednesday before Holy Week. Bill's life-long interest in Biblical archeology had been rewarded with a personal discovery that would not only have archeologists and historians salivating, but it would have repercussions throughout the entire Christian world.

He had called to make sure that it was okay to come at this time, and was glad to see Sarah sitting on the enclosed porch of the rectory, waiting for him. Her sister had arrived, fixed supper for the two of them, and was in the kitchen cleaning up and washing dishes.

"Oh, Daniel, thanks for coming. You didn't have to. I'm being well taken care of already."

"Of course I had to. Bill and you and I have been friends for a long time."

Though her face was still a bit reddened and there were moist tissues on the table next to her, she smiled, "Yes, and you had me before he did." She motioned for him to join her on the porch bench.

It had been years since either of them had made reference to the fact that Sarah and Danny had dated before the older Bill had come back to school for graduate studies in archeology. Their romance had been passionate, but he had never experienced true love until he later met, dated, and married his late wife Samantha. Sarah, meanwhile, had her head turned when the two of them met Bill at a campus peace rally their senior year. Sarah had always had an unerring ability to recognize money, and Bill's family had always had a lot of it. At first the three of them went together to the hunt races at the fabulous Mellon estate near Ligonier. Soon Sarah and Bill were hand-in-hand at upper crust events without him. Their wedding the next year was one of the high society events of that season, and Danny had been best man.

Even veteran pastors as skilled as Danny, can be left not knowing what to say. The combination of the tragedy earlier that morning and her surprise reference to their long ago romance rendered him speechless. He let it slide by without reply.

"You holding up okay?"

"I guess. I can't really get my head around why Bill would do this. It just doesn't make sense. It really helps to have Sally here. And your being here." She smiled, a bit weepy, and leaned over to put her head on his shoulder.

He put an arm around her gently. "I know none of this makes sense. It doesn't for me, either. But I'm here for you. Anything I can do, tell me, or call me later. Anything at all."

"They said they expect to release the body after the medical examiner finishes with it tomorrow. The funeral director will pick it up and take it to the mortuary. I'll need to find out when his brother and my family can all get here, but the funeral service will be at Church the Resurrection, of course, with interment immediately following. The bishop and all the diocese staff will be there, with the bishop officiating by necessity. But will you give a eulogy after?"

"I'd be honored. Of course I will. I'll coordinate with them at the Diocese Office. Do you want me to be there when you go to the mortuary for arrangements?" He knew how stressful that experience could be.

"No, that won't be necessary. Sally will go with me Tuesday morning. And my brother Ken will probably be here by then. He thinks he can get a bereavement reservation scheduled for tomorrow from Houston."

"Good. But let me know if you change your mind. If not, and if you don't mind, I think I'll stop by the precinct headquarters that morning, just to make sure all's in order on their end."

Sarah smiled. "Thanks. I'd appreciate that." She hugged him again and he left.

As he drove back home, Danny continued to mull over his observations about the strange little bit of cord and the choke tube. He hadn't said anything about them to Sarah because he thought he was probably just being his obsessive self and seeing possible "evidence" when it was nothing.

CHAPTER EIGHT

The next morning, the Monday after Easter, Danny went out on his patio with his after-breakfast cup of coffee and sat down again in his usual Adirondack chair. Monday was his customary day off from church work, so he had slept in. He woke stewing about the shotgun choke tube and the multi-colored, frayed cord on Bill's study floor. The more he thought about it, the more he convinced himself that the twisted cord had to have come from a friendship bracelet belonging to someone who was both an old antagonist and an old friend. Will "Tiny" Jones.

It was an old, worn-out custom to nickname a particularly tall, massive man "Tiny." But Tiny Jones had been known almost exclusively by that for most of his years, ever since he had towered over his grade school classmates in the "hood" where he grew up. He played defensive tackle for the Pitt Panthers when he had carried 322 pounds on his 6'5" frame, and like most college football stars, he had hopes of going pro in the NFL. But vulnerable knees and slowness of foot dashed those plans. Upon leaving the university without finishing a degree, like too many college football players, Tiny had returned to his native "turf" in the old, African-American slum ghetto called the Hill.

It was on the Hill that Danny met Tiny. Their relationship began with a rough start. Danny was a newly-ordained minister, out of the Pittsburgh Theological Seminary in Highland Park, and his first parish had been the multiracial congregation at New Life Community Church. In the early 1960's the little Presbyterian church in the ghetto was a brave mission experiment ministering to the heavily black community, while seeking to include at least some whites, Asian-Americans, and one family of Native Americans.

One day in the first week of his pastorate at New Life, Danny had been unpacking boxes of books in his new Pastor's Study when his doorway had been completely filled by the giant form of Tiny. A bit startled and a little bit apprehensive, Danny rose quickly to greet this unexpected visitor.

"Hi," he said, extending his hand, "I'm Reverend Henriks. I'm the new pastor here."

"I don't care who you are, fool," came a snarling reply. "You don't belong here, whitey. So don't you be out on my streets messing with my boys."

Danny was soon to learn that Tiny was a feared gang leader who intimidated residents and shop owners. Many of the shop owners paid protection money to Tiny. Even police officers on patrol were wary of him and his gang.

More than once officers had brought Tiny in on some charge like possession of an illegal substance, carrying a concealed weapon without a permit, and each time more than one officer had had to receive medical treatment as a result of the resisted arrest. Tiny had been incarcerated for each resisted arrest, but the original "bust" charges had never stuck to him. The gang leader had excellent legal representation.

As a very intentional mission outreach to the ghetto community, New Life Community Church always had multiple programs operating involving the people of the Hill. Some were genuinely non-controversial, like summer *Vacation Bible School* and street fairs or recreation for the area children. Others were highly controversial, like *Turn in Your Weapons*, jointly sponsored with the Pittsburgh Police Department. Another, *Alternatives to Gangs* involved counseling, mentoring, job training, and other services to give young boys and men just what the name said. To Tiny those programs were not merely controversial, but they were unacceptable threats to his business and status.

"I mean it, fool," Tiny had growled with an ominously pointed finger and thumb, like a pointed gun. "Just repack those books and get out of here. Now!" And light from the hall outside Danny's study poured back in as the huge form blocking it wheeled and left.

Danny had been grateful back then that no one was in the church at the time to enter and see his visibly shaken body slump into his desk chair. Pittsburgh Theological Seminary was a fine institution for theological education, but it had never prepared him for the likes of Tiny in his pastoral ministry. He wondered if it was too late to reconnect with that pastor nominating/search committee from Montana.

However, Danny was both idealistic and trusting enough in what he hoped was the protection of guardian angels. It would require an entire squadron of them in this environment.

He stayed.

Despite prompting the programs for alternatives to gangs and weapon turn-ins, he quickly gained a well-deserved reputation for caring about and helping the people on the Hill.

Tiny gradually transitioned from menacing glares when they were within viewing distance of each other on a street, to ignoring him entirely, to one day a grudging nod in his direction. Tiny may have been a feared gang leader, but he was genuinely concerned about "his people" in the neighborhood, and he recognized when they were being benefited and not exploited.

Danny knew their uneasy relationship turned a real corner early one evening. He walked alone to his car after locking the church after a council meeting. Three young thugs stopped him. One was in front, blocking his access to his car, the other two in back, cutting off any thoughts of retreat.

"Hey, preacher man," the one in front said, "where ya off to this fine evening?"

"Just going to my car, heading home."

"Well, you won't be needing your wallet and watch for this trip now, will you?" The leader's threatening voice was simultaneously matched by the appearance of a switchblade in his hand. "Hand 'em over, real slow like."

Suddenly a massive shadow had stepped out of the darkness at the edge of the parking lot. A now familiar voice boomed out, "Leroy, it's mighty neighborly of you to be helping the pastor to his car, but I have it from here. You go now. Find someone else to escort."

The local high school track coach would have been impressed at the speed at which the three thugs sprinted out of there. Nobody messed with Tiny, who had disappeared before the again-shaken Danny could even utter a word of thanks.

CHAPTER NINE

The next year brought a growing tolerance that led to real protection and culminated in actual friendship with Tiny when Danny found himself on an ad hoc citizens advisory group the Mayor's Office had formed to "advise" on proposed re-urbanization of part of the Hill. In what seemed from the beginning as a cliché, Danny was recruited as the Protestant minister for the group. Monsignor O'Malley was the Catholic priest from the Diocese of Pittsburgh, and Rabbi Lapin was appointed from a nearby synagogue.

Remarkably, Tiny was a member of the group along with other public figures from the Hill community. He had spent the last few years re-inventing himself and his "boys" from street gang thugs to African-American "businessmen." The Mayor's Office had practically salivated at the opportunity to place a "reformed," previously-incarcerated, public enemy, now a respected, legitimate community business leader, on their showcase committee. The media wouldn't fail to pick up on such an outstanding success on the part of the mayor's rehabilitation of offenders program.

It didn't matter that while some of Tiny's business ventures were, in fact, mostly legitimate, there were other, less visible, activities that remained highly illegal. For example, there was the lucrative, low-effort protection service for Hill stores and shops, as well as the honoraria paid to patrol officers that both relieved them from having to investigate the protection scheme and kept them from further altercations with the giant, partially-reformed businessman.

It didn't take long for Danny, Tiny, and other Hill representatives to recognize the true purpose of their advisory group. The mayor's administration had worked behind the scenes for a long time to address "urban blight" and was ready to reveal their plan to demolish numerous blocks of the Hill. They would offer the land at bargain prices to eager developers to build a mall, professional offices, and several condos and townhouses for a more upscale citizenry.

The location was a relatively short distance from downtown Pittsburgh. The plan included a vastly improved public transportation, replacing the decrepit old city bus service. Of course, it also provided solid security services to shield the elaborate development from less desirable elements there on the Hill.

The publicity was well-orchestrated to celebrate the ground-breaking advances in re-urbanization this development promised. Additionally, it removed a good deal of the blight from the Hill. The citizens of the advisory group were expected to proclaim this redevelopment as a win for everyone, with appropriate media coverage, of course.

The slick presentation paused for "please, tell us more" encouragement and eager questions from the advisory citizens from the Hill. For a few seconds there was stunned silence as Danny, Tiny, and the others looked at each other, at the mayor's head table, at the cameras and microphones around the edges of the conference room. Even the anything but shy Tiny seemed temporarily at a loss for words. The mayor himself broke the increasingly uncomfortable quiet.

"Who has the first question about this great proposal?" he asked with his best politician's practiced smile.

"I do," Danny mustered the simple courage to speak up. "If this highly profitable, commercial development were to take place, what would happen to the hundreds of people who live there now? Where would they go?"

Clearly not anticipating a question of this sort, nor anything else but positive response, the mayor displayed a hint of fluster and annoyance as he dismissively replied, "Well, somewhere else, I suppose."

In those few words, the proverbial cat was out of the bag. The city administration had not given any thought to the fact that hundreds, maybe even thousands, of people lived, worked, got sick, and died in those vermin-infested tenement houses and apartments that would be torn down. At least, no thought beyond the potential for a desirable development after the population was removed.

The Hill citizen representatives erupted in loud protest. Tiny looked so ominously angry that Danny had no trouble picturing the mayor being the next to be treated at the nearest trauma center.

The television and radio people, who easily outnumbered all others in the room, dove into action like sharks. In the background of the melee Danny had already heard reporters' lead-ins, "Live from the Mayor's Office, today's presentation on a new development project for the Hill has collapsed into chaos."

A rapid adjournment was called, repeatedly, over the volcanic hubbub. Presumably the mayor's real advisors had retreated to lick their wounds and retool their plans.

As he left the conference room, Danny had smiled just slightly at the thought that the next time re-urbanization of the Hill was proposed, it would probably not include a citizens advisory group, or at least certainly not him.

As he walked down the marble steps of City Hall, Tiny caught up to him, completely enveloped him with a hug that would have done an Alaska brown bear proud.

"Thanks, man, you laid those bastards bare with your question. We all owe you, brother."

"No, Tiny," Danny replied with genuine sincerity, "my life and work and friends are just as much at stake here as anybody else. You don't owe me anything. But thanks, I appreciate it."

And that had started a friendship between them that was permanent, fierce in its loyalty.

The bond provided the additional benefit that Danny could walk down a dark alley at midnight in the Hill with a fistful of

Franklins waving above his head, and nobody would do anything more than greet him in passing with, "Good evening, pastor, God bless you."

Some of Tiny's protection service, like others of his businesses, was really legitimate.

The day after the mayor's aborted meeting and press conference, as the political blood spread through the airways of the media, Tiny had shown up again to fill his study door. They started to get to know each other on a much more personal level as good friends. Danny gave Tiny one of the intricately-woven, twisted, multi-colored friendship bracelets that were a craft project there at New Life Community Church.

Tiny never took it off.

CHAPTER TEN

Before lunchtime arrived Monday, Danny was back in his Grand Cherokee and headed up to Shadyside to Church of the Resurrection. Just to be sure, he wanted to retrieve that little piece of friendship bracelet. If he could verify that that's what it was, it would be strong evidence that Tiny had been in Bill Brand's study. And while Danny couldn't believe that Tiny would be involved in Bill's death, it might be worthwhile to look Tiny up and ask him about it.

The question nagged at him. Why else would Tiny have been there? Bill and Tiny were certainly not friends. Quite the contrary. After the fiasco regarding the old mayor's re-urbanization plans for the Hill, reporters in the Pittsburgh area had engaged in a feeding frenzy, running around interviewing any public figure they could about the spreading scandal. City council members had microphones shoved in their faces, accompanied by inflammatory questions like "Where do you stand on the mayor's plans to kick citizens of the Hill from their homes and apartments?"

One of the religious leaders interviewed about the mess had, in fact, been his good friend Bill Brand. The rector of one of the most prestigious churches in the Greater Pittsburgh area had appeared on television being questioned about the proposed Hill redevelopment. It didn't surprise Danny that Bill had sided with the mayor. After all, wealthy members of Bill's congregation were almost certainly to be involved, if not directly, at least financially, in the billions of dollars that would be necessary to get the entire project accomplished. Many of Bill's people would undoubtedly stand to make a lot of money.

Bill's face appeared on the evening news, and his deep pulpit voice had pronounced that "It is shameful that the mayor is being pilloried because of his visionary plan to revitalize a cancerous section of our beloved city."

Tiny had gone ballistic. Another television reporter had caught up to him as one of the representatives from the Hill community on the advisory group and had thrown verbal gasoline on the raging fire of the controversy. "What did you think of the Rev. Dr. Brand's reference to the Hill as a cancer in the city?"

Diplomacy had never been Tiny's forte, nor political rhetoric for that matter, and goaded too much, he had growled back, "If this man believes himself to be a man of God, maybe he'd like to meet God sooner rather than later."

That scandal and hubbub had dissipated long ago. New mayors had come and gone. Hardly anyone but someone like Danny would remember who said what. And if Tiny had felt murderous about it, why wait this long to exact punishment against Bill for his siding with the mayor and the big money people?

Danny pulled into the Church of the Resurrection's parking lot for the second time in as many days. It was a very different scene. Gone were the official cars, the flashing lights, and the yellow tape at the side door going into the hall where the Rector's Study was located. Danny stopped by the Church Office to ask permission to look in Bill's study for a moment. He found Margaret, the longtime Church Secretary, talking with Father Frank Lewis, Bill's young Assistant Rector. They were going over the invitations and detailed preparations for the funeral service to be held there for Bill on Friday of that week. Their faces looked lined with grief and fatigue.

"I'm so sorry to bother you both," Danny began, "but I wondered if it would be okay for me to step into the Rector's Study for just a moment. I was there yesterday morning, and I fear that I absentmindedly set down my favorite sunglasses when I was talking with Sergeant Bradley."

"Dr. Henriks, come in; it's good to see you," Father Frank brightened slightly. "Margaret, let's take a brief break. Please make some of those calls while I walk Dr. Henriks down to Dr. Brand's study."

"I hope it's not too much trouble."

"Not at all. We can use a breather from all this stress. I'm afraid the cleaning crew didn't turn in any sunglasses, however. With the sergeant's permission, we had an emergency cleaning service come over already this morning. The big Persian rug has been removed; everything scrubbed and vacuumed; the stained glass window behind the desk sanitized. You wouldn't know the tragedy had even occurred there, but we'll always know, of course...." Frank's voice quavered and trailed off.

As Father Frank opened the door to the Rector's Study, Danny immediately glanced down to the floor below the West African weaving on the wall. Frank had been absolutely right. Everything was spotless. There was no bit of frayed cord on the floor near the baseboard. All had been vacuumed up.

Danny quickly switched mental gears to his little fib about the sunglasses. He made a pretense of looking around the desk, the conference table, counters under the stained glass windows.

"Nope, not here that I can see, Frank. But thanks for allowing me to check. Probably left them in a coffee shop or store yesterday."

"Come back and see us anytime. And you'll be doing a eulogy for the reception after Friday's funeral I understand?"

"Definitely. It's the least I can do for Bill and Sarah."

"See you then." Frank turned and went back to the Church Office.

Danny pulled out of the parking lot brooding about the lost fragment of friendship bracelet. If the church custodian had cleaned and vacuumed, he might have been tempted to sneak into the janitor's closet somehow and empty out the bag to look for it, but with a professional cleaning service, he knew that they would have taken all the dirt and any debris with them. It was probably already disposed of in a dumpster. But still, he felt certain of what he had seen.

His fib about a coffee shop reminded him that it was now lunchtime, so he pulled into one of his favorite places on Baum Boulevard, ordered a venti decaf and a breakfast sandwich, and sat down to think. Was he being foolish, just his typically obsessive self? He decided to check on Sarah.

"Hello." She answered the phone at the rectory right away.

"Sarah, it's Danny. How are you doing?"

"I'm okay, I think. Like they say, hangin' in there. Sally fixed lunch, and she and I are just sitting here in the breakfast nook, talking about arrangements. Are you at home after an exhausting Easter Sunday, which I made even worse?"

"Now don't talk like that. I would have been upset if you hadn't called me and let me come over. Actually I was just at your church. Would it be convenient for me to stop by again in a few minutes? I'm over on Baum."

"Why of course," she responded with enthusiasm. "Sally just made a fresh pot of coffee, but she's about to leave and run some errands. I'm staying home to try to get my bearings and catch my breath before we have to go to the airport later this evening to pick up Ken. Come, have a cup with me."

"Thanks, I'll be right there."

The rectory was on the same block as Church of the Resurrection, over on a back corner, so Danny headed back to the church parking lot, pulling in a stall near the rectory. He had decided that even if he hadn't been able to retrieve the bit of frayed cord, it was only fair to tell Sarah about it.

He also wanted to try to find Tiny and ask him if he'd ever been in Bill's study. Despite Tiny's rough history with gangs, and his ongoing sketchy business dealings, Danny really couldn't see him holding a grudge for so many years as to want to murder Bill now. Besides, there actually was a good heart under that mountainous, intimidating frame.

For some reason, he felt compelled to hold back his doubts about the mysterious choke tube in the shotgun. He knew full well that a despairing, confused mind *could* take the gun out of its safe, remove the snap cap, take the choke tube out of its case, screw it in as though he was going to shoot a round of trap, then go over to the church, into his study, liquor up, and do the deed. But it made no sense for Bill to go to the additional effort to break long-established habit. He shook his head. Sense, he thought, what sense does all this make, anyhow? What sense is it to commit suicide, especially, for someone like Bill?

He decided to wait to bring up yet another crazy idea until his planned stop at the precinct tomorrow. Jim Bradley had indicated that a quick forensics check on the shotgun, examination of the body, and review of notes and photos at the scene could all be wrapped up today, and confirmation of the suicide would be issued Tuesday.

CHAPTER ELEVEN

Sitting with Sarah in her living room, Danny drank a good sip of the freshly-brewed coffee and revealed to her his concern about the now-missing bit of twisted cord.

"It's probably nothing at all, and I probably shouldn't even mention it, especially now that it's been vacuumed up and is undoubtedly irretrievable. But, Sarah, I just can't believe Bill would take his own life. And, although the police wouldn't have anything to go on to follow up on it, I'd just feel better if I could ask Tiny if he had some occasion to be in Bill's study recently."

"Well, I certainly can't believe anything about Bill's death myself. When did you have in mind to go see this Tiny? I want to go, too," she said with determination.

"Oh, Sarah, you have more than enough to do with the funeral at the end of this week. As I said, it's probably nothing but my usual compulsiveness. Besides, Tiny's office is still in a pretty rough part of the Hill. He may be involved in legitimate businesses these days, but he's always considered the slum to be his home, and the people there to be his people."

"I don't care," Sarah's voice rose. "If there's *any* possibility of Bill's death being other than suicide, I insist upon finding out. I want you to take me there. When are we going?"

Going back to their days together as lovers in school, Danny had no trouble recognizing when Sarah had made up her mind and there was no changing it. He might as well save his breath. He thought a second.

"I told you yesterday that I wanted to stop by the precinct to see Sergeant Bradley tomorrow morning. I'll try to call around this afternoon about Tiny's whereabouts, if he's going to be in his office Tuesday afternoon, and if so, we could go then if it works for you."

"Perfect. Later this afternoon I'm going to go over to our...my..." she corrected with a slight catch in her throat, "health club and get in a few laps. I have never needed to unwind and relax as much as right now. There's the mortuary tomorrow morning, lunch with Sally and Ken, but I can get away when you want to go to the Hill in the afternoon. Ken and Sally will get to making more phone calls, arrange for flowers, and pick away at all the details remaining. I'll just tell them that you and I have a special errand we have to do."

Danny was glad to hear her mention going to the health club.

"Swimming a few laps will be good for you. I remember that it's always been one of your favorite ways to relax."

Sarah had been on the Pitt swim team as an undergrad. She had always kept up with her swimming, was marvelously toned and fit, and, frankly, was a head-turner when out on the town. It wasn't a lack of beauty or passion that kept her from being The One. He didn't even mind her bossy determination and occasional hardheadedness. She just didn't turn out to be his soul mate and partner for life. They were good together as a couple, but it had been Samantha who had completed him, and he – her.

He left her, but not before she gave him a hug at her door that reminded him of those old days. Rather than the polite, social, lean forward and *mwah* at the cheek, she embraced him hard, enabling him to feel all the arousing softness and lean hardness of that great body. He felt awkward about it, but chalked it up to her need of the moment to be held and comforted. So he didn't pull away so as to pass on his awkward feeling, but gently let go of her as soon as he thought he could without offending.

Danny drove back home to make calls and try to get a fix on Tiny for Tuesday afternoon.

CHAPTER TWELVE

He had called the police station and found out that Detective Sergeant Bradley would be in by 9:00 a.m., so Danny first stopped by South Presbyterian. There he found Tim Murphy and their Church Secretary, Mildred, in the Church Office. Mildred was used to him being in by 8:00, as soon as the church opened for the day.

"Tim, do you suppose you could take the sermon and lead the services this coming Sunday? And Mildred, would you please call Jack, our personnel chair, and tell him that I'm going to take the rest of this week as vacation. I have four weeks coming this year, and something's come up that requires my immediate attention. He'll probably want you to email and/or send postcards to all the elders so that everybody's informed. It shouldn't be a problem since it's not unusual for me to take some time off after the hectic Lenten/Easter season."

"Glad to do it," Tim replied, and Mildred in her typical efficiency said that she'd get right on it.

She asked Danny, "Will you be staying at home and should I call if there's a death in the congregation?"

Almost everything else could be covered by Tim, including any hospital emergencies, and Danny could be filled in with anything that happened while he was taking this break, but his usual policy was to be called immediately – even if he was on the other side of the country – whenever a death occurred. For most people, that was a time when they wanted quick contact from their pastor, even if they were fine with Reverend Murphy doing the funeral service. There were a few times, however, when he had left his vacation and traveled back to Pittsburgh to do a funeral. For some folks, a death in the family couldn't be ministered to by anyone other than their pastor.

"So far as I know, I should be home or nearby, but I will be out and about, so use my cell number first. Week after Easter meeting and event schedule is light, so there shouldn't be any balls dropped there. I will be unreachable some of the time, but leave a voice mail if I don't answer, and I'll call in each day for any more urgent messages that might not wait until I'm back in. Otherwise, expect me to show up exactly one week from today. Okay?"

"Yes, sir." Mildred smiled in her unfailing cheerfulness.

Tim gave him a thumbs-up. Tim should be looking for a call to his own pastorate before long, and he'd be glad for the extra preaching opportunity, not only for practice, but also to get more sermons in his proverbial "sermon barrel." When starting at a new church, there was always such a flood of things to do in the first weeks and months that it was extremely helpful to have a file drawer of sermons that could be pulled out, dusted off, and wouldn't require hours and days to develop.

"Oh, and I'll be giving a eulogy after the funeral service at Church of the Resurrection on Friday, probably 11:00 in the morning. Waiting on confirmation from his wife and the funeral director."

"We'll be waiting to hear about that officially and will be sure to let any callers know," Mildred assured.

"And I'll plan on attending," said Tim. Bill and Tim had never had occasion to spend much time together – mostly at monthly ministerial association lunch meetings – but for someone like Bill with his status, a considerable number of area clergy would make it a point to attend, especially, of course, his colleagues from the Episcopal Diocese of Pittsburgh.

"Great," Danny replied. "I'll look for you before the service, and we can plan on sitting in a back pew like good Presbyterians." All three of them chuckled at that one.

CHAPTER THIRTEEN

Back in his Jeep before 9:00, Danny headed over to check in with Jim Bradley, who, sure enough, was in his office, at his desk. The desk sergeant greeted Danny with a welcoming, "Good morning, Chaplain, go right back; he's expecting you."

Sergeant Bradley saw him coming, waved him in, and offered a chair.

"What have you determined, Jim?"

"Suicide, no question. The only prints on the shotgun were his, including where he had grasped the fore piece and barrel to hold it while he stuck the muzzle in his mouth. His prints were the only ones on the bottle of scotch. He had used Dr. Scholl's foot powder on his feet, and there was a trace of that on the trigger and trigger guard from where he had used his big toe to fire the gun. There was absolutely nothing to suggest even the remote possibility of foul play. His blood alcohol level was really elevated, so he was pretty liquored-up to bolster his courage."

"Did you find any suicide note?"

"No, but we did question his wife, of course, who was extremely distraught, and various church staff members, his lay president of his church council, who was there for Easter Sunday service. Nobody shared that he was seriously depressed or acting "off" the weeks before Easter. Apparently he had been experiencing some friction and disagreements regarding proposed church renovations with a few of his trustees, but we couldn't come up with anyone or anything that might lead to anything other than his taking his own life. He didn't seem to have any serious enemies in any aspect of his life and work. Like I said, suicide, open and shut."

And as he had thought about it previously, Danny refrained from any mention of the bit of twisted cord from the friendship bracelet, especially since it couldn't be produced, but also because it wouldn't have seemed relevant to the death, there being no physical evidence of any other person being involved in Bill's violent demise. Neither did he bring up the curious screw-in of the choke tube. Again, even if to put them in away from the gun range was something Bill just didn't do, it didn't mean that he could not have....and there were no finger prints other than Bill's. Still, for Danny, it would have been an act that didn't make sense.

"Well, thanks, Jim, for sharing your findings with me. Oh, will you be releasing the gun back to his wife?"

"Sure, there's no reason for us to have it. She can pick it up any time later this week."

"Or if she gives me written authorization, would it be all right for me to get it for her? Under the circumstances, she might not want to touch it even."

"I see no problem with that. Tomorrow or later this week, after notes are reviewed and finalized."

It disturbed Danny that everyone – even Sarah, actually – seemed prepared to accept the death as a straightforward suicide. Maybe it was just his exaggerated denial of the facts of the matter. Nonetheless, after lunch he would drive over to the Hill and look up his old nemesis-turned-fierce-friend, Tiny, and against his wishes, he'd take Sarah with him.

CHAPTER FOURTEEN

Danny picked Sarah up at the rectory, and they drove west toward the Hill District. In the era of the 1930's to 50's, the Hill had often been referred to as "Little Harlem." Historically it had been considered the cultural center of African-Americans in Western Pennsylvania. One of the famous jazz clubs in that era had been owned and operated by Gus Greenlea.

For a time, Pittsburgh Pirates Hall-of-Fame slugger Willie Stargell had owned a fried chicken shop in the Hill, and any customers who happened to be in the store at the time that Willie hit a home run in a Pirates game would be given free fried chicken. The store was very popular during ball games. Despite the fried chicken benefit, at least half of the residents of the Hill lived below the poverty line.

Re-urbanization, urban renewal, economic development, displacing some 8000 people to build the Civic Arena – whatever it was called, whatever was done, the urban blight that had concerned the mayor back when Danny and Tiny were citizen "advisors" was persistent to a high degree of frustration. Most important, people were born in poverty on the Hill, lived, died prematurely far too often, and were mostly trapped without dreams or hopes.

Danny had found out that Tiny still operated an "office" in one of the squalid apartments of Bedford Terrace, which was officially packed with 7000 residents per square mile....but in reality probably a lot more who escaped being counted. He parked near the building he had been told about, and Sarah and he approached warily. And while Danny had never been the least bit racist – which had contributed greatly to the acceptance he had won while being pastor of New Life Church – mere observation found that their two faces were the only white ones visible. Their entrance into the building was watched suspiciously....and maybe opportunistically.

He asked the first person he encountered near the bank of mailboxes – more than one of which were smashed – about Tiny Jones' apartment, and received a quick nod up the stairs. There was no functioning elevator.

Outside, Tuesday afternoon after Easter was again bright and sunny, but by the time they reached the third floor, the hallway was amazingly dark, dingy, and frankly ominous. Not as ominous, however, as the two tall African-American men who stepped in front of them from one of the open doors and took a threatening stance.

"You lost or somethin'? You don't belong here."

"We're here to see Tiny," Danny quickly explained. "I called him yesterday."

Sarah added, "We just want to talk to him."

"He's not in," one of the big men growled. "Get lost."

But before Danny could protest, further explain, or think better of their situation and turn to leave, a smashing blow to the back of his head turned everything black. Falling unconscious, he had no awareness that the man who had snuck up behind them grabbed his ankles, one in front grabbed under his arms, and the third grabbed Sarah roughly, pinning her arms from behind.

CHAPTER FIFTEEN

Danny gradually emerged from the blackness with a throbbing head, blurry vision, and someone patting his cheek more gently than his previous encounter would have indicated. As he tried feebly to focus, he heard the long-familiar voice of Tiny.

"Okay, he's coming out of it now. Danny, can you hear me? Are you okay?"

Okay was definitely not the word Danny would have chosen. His head was splitting – undoubtedly a concussion – and he hadn't felt so woozy since a player near the size of Tiny had blindsided him during an intramural football game many years ago.

"Tiny...." he started, but quickly redirected his utterance in another direction, "Sarah, where's Sarah?" Danny jerked his head around the "office" and spotted her sitting in a chair, her hair mussed, a bit disheveled, her top slightly torn at the neckline....but otherwise, as best as he could see with his dizziness, she seemed okay, though her face was reddened again with tears and anxiety.

"I'm okay, Daniel. They didn't hurt me."

On the opposite side of the room, the tough guy who had grabbed her in the hallway was looking down at the floor sullenly, his visible cheek itself reddened by a punch from someone. The other two appeared actually sheepish, keeping their distance from both Sarah and Danny.

"Nah," inserted Tiny, "my boys did her no harm. But I had to apply a little corrective action. That was no way to treat my visitors, especially such a fine lady. I'm afraid they had been out on business for me, hadn't heard about my approval of your coming, and thought you might be narc undercover cops or something....or even worse, Jehovah's Witness." At which Tiny exploded in laughter, and even Danny was tempted to chuckle....or at least might have if his head hadn't felt like it was exploding.

"Slick, get our guests something to drink. Beer, coffee, soda pop?" he turned to Danny and glanced at Sarah. The big fellow with the reddened cheek rose attentively, seemingly repentant for his rough handling of Sarah.

"Coffee if you have it," Danny replied with a slightly less shaky voice. Maybe some caffeine would help clear the cobwebs. Sarah, obviously still upset and afraid, shook her head to decline. Cup soon in hand, Danny proceeded to bring Tiny up to speed on the aftermath of Bill's death.

"Yah, I heard about Dr. Brand's death on the news yesterday," Tiny responded. "I was real sorry to hear it. When him and me first met, I thought he was just another wealthy big shot covering the asses of his big shot friends, but he proved me wrong."

Danny told him about the little piece of frayed, twisted friendship bracelet that he had seen in Bill's study Easter Sunday morning. He omitted the part of it having been vacuumed up and certainly lost forever.

"It had to have come from yours," Danny gestured to the friendship bracelet that hung as always on Tiny's right wrist. "Each one we made at New Life was unique in colors and style. But how could it have gotten into Bill's study?"

"Oh, man, I hope you don't think that I had anything to do with his death. Sure, when he was interviewed on television that time years ago, I was mad big time about the way he talked about the Hill being a cancer, acting like the people there didn't matter, talking like some whitey racist. But all that changed; we came together on all that."

Her mood lifted by now, Sarah jumped in. "I'm Dr. Brand's wife. What changed between the two of you?"

"Dang, Mrs. Brand, that makes me feel even badder about

Slick and the boys being rough with you. We're sorry about that." Slick and the other two nodded with unusual enthusiasm. Whatever Tiny said, that was the way it would be.

Tiny answered her question. "Maybe a couple of weeks after that interview, Dr. Brand called me. Somehow he had gotten my office number here. He asked if I would be willing to come to his office, that he wanted to apologize for his stupid remarks, and that he had something to give me, if I would accept it. I suspected that if he was feeling pressure from the media controversy, maybe he wanted to buy me off, get me and my boys to back off from speaking to reporters about him....or from opposing that development project. I told him that he could keep whatever he had for me....and that I didn't belong in fancy Shadyside anymore than his bullshit belonged on the air about the Hill."

"So what brought the two of you together?" Danny asked.

"Well, he insisted, and he seemed sincere about it. He said that I had every right to be in Shadyside as much as he did, that I would be his personal guest, so I went one day. He apologized to me in front of his office staff, admitted that he hadn't thought out his comments well enough, that he had sinned before God, everyone who had heard that interview and the people here on the Hill; and he wanted to make amends. I recognized what he was doing from my twelve-step program – NA – when I got clean and sober myself."

Sarah added, "Yes, Bill was a recovering alcoholic – going back to his Pitt days, when he was trying to numb the pressure of grad school. But he was convinced that he could control it now, and still loved his expensive scotch."

"Well, I accepted his apology. And then he said it would be a giant favor if I could find it in me to accept the envelope he handed me."

"What was it?"

"It was a check for $10,000 from the church local mission fund. He was quick to assure me that he was not trying to buy my silence, but that when he realized the foolishness and hurtfulness of his comments, he had convinced his rich trustees that it was long overdue for them to contribute to the Hill rather than condemn it. The money was for the summer youth programs, to give Hill kids like here at Bedford Terrace good things to do when out on summer break."

"But what about the fragment of your friendship bracelet?

"Oh, yah," Tiny said, holding up his right hand and pointing to the bracelet. "As you can see, it's pretty worn. Well, last week he called me again like he has every year during Holy Week to give me another check for the summer program starting in a couple of months. He always wanted it kept quiet, though."

"Sure," Danny agreed, "not because he was embarrassed about giving to you guys, but because of Church of the Resurrection's 'Give in Secret' Lenten program – that Jesus talked about in the Beatitudes – give in secret and the Father who sees in secret will reward you."

"Yah, yah, that's it! That's just the way Dr. Brand told it. Anyway, I went – this time in his own office – and before I left, we hugged as friends. And you see how the ends of my bracelet are knotted to keep the twist from unraveling. Well, the knot on one end caught on his wrist watch and easily snapped off. No harm to the watch, but I didn't see where the end went to. That's what you saw on the floor."

"What day was that?" asked Sarah.

"Ah, last Wednesday. 'Cause he said that Thursday and Friday were busy days for him with services and stuff."

"Makes sense – Holy Thursday and Good Friday. And the church custodian wouldn't have cleaned and vacuumed his study until Monday usually, on Bill's regular day off."

Danny's head was clearing by now, the ache more annoying than disabling. He suggested to Sarah that the two of them get going.

"Okay," she agreed. "But I'm driving. If you have a concussion, no way I'm taking a chance on you blacking out again behind the wheel." He might have protested that he was fit to drive, but he could tell that, once again, her mind was made up.

Tiny was quick to add, "And I'm really sorry for both of you getting mistreated like that. Sometimes my protection services can get a little too protective, you know?" And he roared in laughter once more. This time Danny managed a smile at least. "Boys, shake hands with our guests and let 'em know how sorry you are about the misunderstanding."

The big bruisers – led by the obedient Slick – stepped forward in turn to offer their hands and "Sorry, man; sorry, ma'am." Danny's head would be sorrier than they for the next few days.

CHAPTER SIXTEEN

They left the Hill, to drive back to Shadyside. It was getting near suppertime and Danny asked Sarah, "Do you want to stop for a bite to eat, or do you need to get back home for Ken and Sally?"

"I'll give them a call and let them know that we'll be a bit longer. They'll be fine. Sally's settled right into the kitchen at the rectory. She'll fix something for the two of them."

"What say we get nostalgic and go to Smallman Street Deli in Squirrel Hill. Remember the great hot pastrami sandwiches we used to get there when we were dating?" Danny suggested.

Squirrel Hill had always had a large Jewish community, and many thought Smallman's had the best corned beef and pastrami west of New York City.

"Sounds terrific," Sarah smiled with eagerness. She had brushed her hair back in place, splashed a little cold water on her previously red face, and looked sensational again, despite the small tear in her top.

They hadn't said much on the drive out of the Hill, mostly making sure that they were okay and settling down from their rough experience outside Tiny's office.

Finally Sarah asked, "What do you think? Was Tiny telling the truth? Or do you think he might have had something to do with Bill's death?"

"Well, it was unusual timing. His being in Bill's study just days before Bill died. Then that piece of Tiny's friendship bracelet being snapped off and was left on the floor. And, they did have a past history of conflict. But, yeah, what he said rings true to me. It makes sense. One thing about Tiny I learned over the years, he's been true to his word. So yes, I believe he told us the truth."

"I do, too. I like him, actually. And his 'protection' seemed genuinely sorry about the way they roughed us up. Your head cleared enough to be able to chew on hot pastrami?" She smiled and parked on Murray Avenue, down the street from Smallman's.

They took a booth at the deli and before long they both had positively giant sandwiches clutched in their hands. The deli was crowded, bustling, and noisy as usual, but even so, Sarah leaned a little closer and spoke in a low voice, "Since we don't regard Tiny as complicit in any way in Bill's death, do you now think it was a suicide like the police concluded?"

"I'm sorry, Sarah," Danny apologized. "I know we both want this to be settled. Especially you, of course. And, you should be spending your time and energy on Friday's funeral service preparations. Be able to grieve. Find closure."

Danny hesitated before continuing "I'm undoubtedly exacerbating the pain you have to be feeling. Maybe for no good reason. But, I still wonder about the shotgun. Sergeant Bradley said I could pick it up for you, if you gave written permission for them to release it to me."

"Of course, but I don't want it. I never liked Bill's hobby with shooting, although I know it was something the two of you did together occasionally. What do you want it for?"

"That was another thing that seemed 'off' to me in the study early Sunday morning. Bill was very particular about his handling of his guns. He always waited until he got to the range house at the gun club before he removed the trigger lock and screwed in the choke tube he planned on using. If he wanted to use it to commit suicide, there would have been no reason to go to the effort to screw in a choke tube first."

"But what is this, this...'choke tube' you call it?"

"Yes, it screws in the muzzle of the shotgun and constricts the hundreds of shot pellets as they exit the barrel when the gun is fired. For longer-range shots, the choke is tighter – holding the string of pellets closer together in a bunch, so that when they get out to the target they aren't spread out so thinly as to enable the target to fly right through the pattern without breaking. For closer range shots, the choke would be less constricting. More 'open'. But range didn't matter on Sunday morning, so why bother with the choking."

Sarah shuddered. "I didn't know about all that. I never paid attention to what he did with his guns. So what will you do?"

"Well, I'm sure you knew that when he and I would go on a Saturday to shoot, we went to the Keystone Rod & Gun Club. That private member club in Hannastown. I haven't been there since after Christmas and New Year's, but I know Bill shot there this spring, so I can check with the range master in the range house and see if he might have observed Bill uncasing his trap gun with the choke tube already screwed in. Maybe he changed his habit and just didn't bother to remove it Sunday morning. If it was already in, why bother taking it out? So maybe he didn't."

Danny paused a minute. "But what troubles me the most is why he would take his life in the first place. I can't see the reason."

"I'm just so angry with him for leaving me like this," Sarah finally admitted. "Whether he did it himself for some unknown reason or someone did it to him, I feel abandoned."

For the first time that day the tears returned.

Danny waited for a moment until she wiped her eyes. "Well, the police don't see the need to look into it any further. But if you don't mind too much, could there be anyone, anyone at all, who would have wanted him dead? If Tiny wasn't an enemy, was there anyone else?"

"It's hard to imagine." Sarah replied. "I mean, sure he had disagreements with people. He was certain that the Roman Catholic Diocese of Pittsburgh would be most unhappy with his ancient text discovery on his trip a couple of years ago to the Holy Land. And probably some really right-wing, conservative Christian groups would get fussed up. But it hadn't actually been publicly announced or published yet."

"I know. That was what he was so ecstatic about when I met with him in his study the week before Holy Week. He had gotten both the final carbon 14 dating, and word from *Biblical*

Archeology that they would feature his text and article on the front page of their monthly magazine. He was certain that *Time,* the major newspapers, of course internet news, would all pick up on it. It was the crowning achievement of his lifelong interest in biblical archeology. All the more reason he had to rejoice in life, not end it."

Darkness had fallen outside by the time they left Smallman's. Danny convinced Sarah that he was okay now, not even groggy, and was soon behind the wheel.

Sarah called to check on Sally and Ken and let them know that Danny and she were finally on the way back to the rectory. But when she reached Sally on her cell, Sally shared that Ken and she had decided to go out themselves, relax with a late dinner, and wouldn't be back until late.

CHAPTER SEVENTEEN

Sarah insisted that Danny come in for a cup of coffee before heading back to his South Hills house. Her sad mood from Smallman's had gone away. She turned on a kitchen light and as they entered the rectory through the kitchen door, she again pressed close to him, gave him a warm kiss on his cheek and an embrace, and whispered loudly with her mouth close to his ear,

"I'm glad you're with me through all this. Thank you." She smiled with bright eyes now as she turned to peer in his.

Sarah looked like she wanted to kiss him again, but a noise came from the direction of Bill's downstairs study at home. With only the kitchen light on, the rest of the house was dark.

Danny pushed Sarah behind him.

"Stay here, I'll check it out."

He ran in the direction of the study just in time to see a figure of a man, dressed all in black, with a black hood over his face and head. The figure dashed toward and out the front door. Danny followed and saw the hooded person disappear behind the shrubbery near the sidewalk. The intruder jumped into a small, light green subcompact car and took off.

Back inside, Danny found Sarah standing at the open door of the study, the ceiling light on now, her mouth agape at the floor covered with files, books, papers, and overturned desk drawers. Somebody had been ransacking the study between the time that Ken and Sally had left and Danny and Sarah had returned. While one could suppose that it had been a simple burglary, all the evidence covering the floor spoke to someone desperately searching for something.

In light of their recent conversation over pastrami sandwiches, Danny grabbed Sarah's arm and turned her gently. "Sarah, do you know where Bill kept that ancient text fragment?"

"Yes," she replied, shakily again. "There's a hidden compartment in the back of the large bottom drawer of his desk, on the right side. It's small, so without taking the drawer out and measuring it against the drawer on the left, you wouldn't even know it was there. And there's a little lever hidden in the side that looks like part of the trim and opens the compartment."

"Would you mind checking?"

Sarah flipped the hidden lever, and the compartment opened. It was empty. If the burglar had found it and opened it, he had closed it again upon taking the contents.

"You may have touched upon who's responsible for both Bill's death and this breaking and entering." Danny told her. "Because even though the man was in black from hooded head to shoes, at his neck I caught a glimpse of a priest's collar. Just a little patch of white. It's hard to believe, but maybe some of the Catholics were more than just a little unhappy with Bill's discovery. And I think I know who to ask about it."

He insisted that she call 911 and have the police investigate for the second time in three days on the grounds of the Church of the Resurrection. He stayed with her until they arrived, and Sally and Ken came home shortly after to find the now all-too-familiar scene of patrol cars and flashing lights. The thought passed through Danny's head that by now the neighbors of the church in the wealthy and normally peaceful area of Shadyside must be wondering what in hell was going on with the Episcopalians over there. The gossip lines would be crackling about this latest, scandalous development.

"You might as well be getting home," Sarah said. "The police will be here for awhile, and Ken and Sally are with me. I'll be okay."

"I was just at the study door," Danny added, "and I watched them looking again for prints or other clues. They are also searching the ground outside for shoe prints, any bit of concrete evidence that might point to the man who was responsible. Hopefully they'll find something. But I guess you're right; I should get going."

Neither of them mentioned anything to the police investigators about the priest's collar. It had been such a split-second glimpse; it was hard to be one hundred percent sure, and Danny wanted to make his own inquiry before putting it out to the police. Not only did everyone know that eyewitness testimony was always questionable, often unreliable, but Danny was also already feeling uneasy about making a fuss about the little piece of friendship bracelet and the choke tube that may or may not mean anything. Besides, there was no way of knowing at this point if there could be any connection whatsoever between Bill's death and the ransacking of his home study.

But as he drove home to South Hills, he knew who he could call. And he would do that Wednesday morning, as soon as the Catholic Diocese office opened.

CHAPTER EIGHTEEN

Danny wanted to make two phone calls after his breakfast Wednesday morning. The first one to the Roman Catholic Diocese of Pittsburgh office at 9:00. The second to the range house at the Keystone Rod & Gun Club when it opened for shooting at 10:00.

Monsignor O'Malley was still on the diocesan staff after all these years, had long been second-in-command to the Bishop of Pittsburgh, and considered Danny a close friend ever since their time together on that mayor's advisory group. The administrative assistant in the diocesan office took his call, told him that the monsignor would be in that morning, and could see him at 11:00.

With almost an hour to kill before he could talk to the range master, Danny sat again in his favorite Adirondack chair on his patio, as always with a cup of hot coffee, and thought about Bill's discovery of a fragment of ancient text.

Bill had made a three-week trip to the Holy Land as a post-Easter vacation about two years ago. As soon as he returned to Pittsburgh, he had called his good friend Danny, excited about something he wanted Danny to see. That same afternoon Danny had stopped by Bill's home study at the rectory, after making a visit to Allegheny General Hospital to see a church member after her surgery.

Bill had Danny sit in one of the fine leather club chairs by his desk, while Bill reached down into a bottom desk drawer. He drew out an old leather packet bound shut by a thong and carefully opened it with such delicate touch that one might have supposed it contained an explosive due to go off. It turned out to be explosive all right, but of a different kind. Bill took a deep breath to calm down, smiled broadly, and began his story.

"I was in an antiquities shop in the Old Section of Jerusalem. I had been there before on previous trips to the Holy Land, had gotten to know the proprietor well, and even corresponded with him from time to time. I had let him know that I was particularly interested in obtaining any old scrap of papyrus text that might come into his hands for my private collection. I assured him that I would pay extremely well for such an item, depending upon what it was, of course, and he knew that I had the money from my family inheritance. Both of us would be most discreet about such a transaction, no one the wiser."

"And I take it he had something for you."

"Yes, he called during Holy Week, as a matter of fact, about a week before I would make my trip there, and said that he had something that might be of interest to me, that I should stop in his shop as soon as I reached Jerusalem. When I did so, he quickly closed the shop and took me into a back room that I had never seen before. He extracted this old leather packet, unfolded it gently, and showed me the fragment of papyrus. Look at it, Danny, but don't remove the protective cover, please, I don't want it exposed to air and moisture here in our more humid climate."

Danny was not the scholar in biblical languages and archeology that Bill was, but he had been an "A" student in several seminary classes at Pittsburgh Theological Seminary in Koine Greek, the language of the New Testament and the time of the apostolic church in the first to second century AD. There was a word, a short phrase, about which he was a little uncertain of the exact translation, but a faded but still legible phrase caught his eye: "*Mary the Magdalene, the wife of Jesus the Christ.*"

"My God, Bill, what is this a fragment of? How old is it? Is it genuine?" The questions spilled out before Bill could utter a word in reply.

"First, Danny, yes, I'm certain it's genuine. Its wording appears in part in the Coptic *Gospel of Mary*, meaning Mary the

Magdalene, but as you would understand, it will have to be tested, put under microscopes, analyzed by the best experts in ancient papyrus writings, compared to verified texts of the same time period. Every kind of scrutiny possible to authenticate it. But I'm certain."

Then almost two years later, the week before this last Easter, a virtually identical scene took place, with Danny occupying the same chair, and Bill once again bringing out the papyrus fragment from that bottom desk drawer.

"I'm pleased and gratified," Bill said, "to be sharing with you today that finally all the tests and analyses have been completed. Carbon 14 dating, microscopic study of the pressed papyrus, analysis of the natural ink used, comparisons with known bits of the Coptic writing. Everything points to this fragment being older than the Coptic book known as *The Gospel of Mary*, probably used in some form by the Coptic scribe, and first century in origin. A Christian contemporary of Jesus Christ, one of the original followers of the Way of Jesus, had to have been the author."

Danny was stunned. Bill's ancient papyrus, with all that scientific and scholarly analysis, had to be regarded as very strong evidence that some of the New Testament scholars of today, historical books, novels, movies or films, particular groups and sects and believers, some condemned as heretics and even put to death by the Church, were right all along! Jesus of Nazareth and Mary of Magdala *were* married, perhaps even had one or more children. It made perfect sense now that *The Gospel According to John* in the canonical New Testament developed such an extensive scene of the Risen Christ appearing to Mary Magdalene on that first Easter Sunday. She was the first witness to the Resurrection among his disciples, and to be a witness to the Resurrection was considered the essential requirement to be an apostle in the earliest Christian community of faith.

Bill went on, "Now that I have all the test results and expert analysis, after Holy week and Easter Sunday, once past all that busyness in the church, we're going to have a press event, with several of my consulting scholars in a panel. There will be a book, of course, and numerous feature articles in first-rate publications like *Biblical Archeology*."

Danny interrupted Bill's beaming, gushing enthusiasm. "But what of the papyrus itself? I'm surprised that you have it here in your study at home."

"Oh, it will go to the Kelso Museum of Near Eastern Archeology at Pittsburgh Theological Seminary. I've been a part of their programs and activities for years. Not only are they so close to us, but they have a long history in biblical and Near Eastern archeology. I've even had an occasional role in a couple of their digs over there. They, of course, have the controlled environment to preserve the papyrus and be able to continue to study it."

"But you didn't house it there up until now?"

"No, you see, something like this is so controversial that I feared it could be vulnerable to theft or being destroyed before we got to this point. I felt better keeping it in secret here until everything was confirmed about its authenticity."

And after Danny left, Bill had with utmost care opened the bottom drawer and replaced it in the desk's hidden compartment. But now Bill was dead, his study ransacked, and the papyrus fragment gone.

Danny roused himself out of his chair. It was 10:00, time to call the range master at the Keystone Rod & Gun Club. Although his suspicions about the possibility of murder remained, he knew that it was possible that Bill's death was actually a suicide, and that the intruder in black who had rummaged through the study was merely looking to steal a highly valuable archeological treasure. Bill had been secretive and protective about his find, but the fact that he had to have scholars and technical experts study the little manuscript over the last almost two years meant that there were people who knew of its existence. And scholars, research people, lab testers, and certainly religious professionals were like virtually everyone else. They talked. They gossiped. And they frankly bragged about their work. The fact that the papyrus existed and was the possession of the Rev. Dr. William Brand had obviously leaked to the wrong person or persons.

CHAPTER NINETEEN

The phone rang and rang at the Keystone range house. Steve, the range master, must be directing the squads of shooters to start the morning, thought Danny. But finally he heard the familiar voice answer.

"Keystone Rod & Gun Club. This is the range house, Steve speaking."

"Steve, hi, it's Daniel Henriks. Have a quick question for you if you have a sec."

"Sure, Dr. Henriks. The first squads have gone out to the shotgun ranges to start. What can I do for you?"

"I wanted to ask you about our late friend, Bill Brand. He was out to shoot a while ago?"

"Oh, yeah," Steve confirmed. "But he only shot a couple of rounds of trap and left again, saying that it was the busy Lenten season for him at his church. Gosh, I was so sorry to hear about his suicide on the news."

"Well, this may seem like an odd question, but did you happen to see him setting up to head out to the trap range? Do you remember at all if he uncased his 1100 and then took a choke tube out and screwed it in? Or did you by any chance see that his gun came out of the case with the choke tube already in place?"

"You know," Steve answered, "Dr. Brand was always one of our really meticulous shooters, always followed good safety protocol, always did things the same way. And a real gentleman, quick to compliment a fellow squad member on a crisp double broken, just as quick to make an excuse for someone's blown shot. You know, like, 'well the wind really caught that target, made it tough for you.' But he was only here that one time this spring, and I just didn't notice about the choke tube. It was his practice, though, to wait 'til just before walking out to the trap range to screw in his choice of tube. But I confess I didn't notice the last time he was here."

"Well, thanks Steve. Just thought I'd ask. Like I said, funny question, but...."

"You know what, though," Steve broke in, "he had also taken an early spring vacation break up to the cottage he and his wife have in Leelanau County, Michigan, and he said that he had gotten in some shooting at the ranges of the club he belongs to there. What was the name of it, ah, Pine Tree, Spruce Tree, something like that, Rod & Gun?"

"Cedar Rod & Gun Club," Danny corrected. "I've never been there with him, but he's shown me lots of photos. Gorgeous area. Mixture of forest, rolling hills, farms, orchards, vineyards, wineries, and lots of water. Lake Michigan on the west side, Grand Traverse Bay on the east, and the Leelanau peninsula full of beautiful lakes. And while the Cedar Club is not your fancy, high-end shooting club, he always said it was a great place to shoot. I know they have some excellent shooters, fine facilities, and John Harrison, possibly the best gun-fitter and stock bender in the country. Maybe I'll check up there about Bill's recent shooting. Thanks for your time, Steve."

"You bet, Dr. Henriks, and come out and break a few clays with us soon, okay?"

"I'll make a point of it. Although my goal would be to break all of them, you know."

They both laughed agreeably on that and said their goodbyes.

CHAPTER TWENTY

Danny drove up toward the Offices of the Roman Catholic Diocese of Pittsburgh. The bishop's seat was in the Cathedral of St. Paul, a towering, gothic-style church, but his friend Monsignor O'Malley had his office among all the other offices of the Administrative Center of the diocese on Boulevard of the Allies, which connected downtown Pittsburgh with the neighborhood of Oakland, home to the University of Pittsburgh and its famed "Cathedral of Learning."

Compulsive about being punctual, along with so many other aspects of his life, Danny reached the receptionist's desk about three minutes before his scheduled appointment with the monsignor. He was ushered right in.

"Danny Henriks," Monsignor O'Malley boomed out with his customary energy. "How have you been? Oh, but what a tragedy, our friend Bill Brand and his suicide. I've been praying for him constantly ever since I heard Sunday evening."

Danny shook his hand, receiving a vigorous pumping in return, and smiled inwardly at the reference to suicide coming from his Catholic friend. Official doctrine was, of course, that suicides were lost souls, not admissible to heaven, but he knew O'Malley well enough to know that the monsignor was more relaxed in his personal beliefs. His prayers for Bill had been sincere, no doubt.

"Yes," Danny replied while taking the offered chair, opposite O'Malley on the other side of a round coffee table. "None of us could believe that Bill would even think, have any reason whatsoever, to take his own life."

"Your own church is not far from his, as I remember."

"Not far at all, though not in as upscale an area as Shadyside. But the closeness enabled me to dash over to Church of the Resurrection early Easter Sunday morning when his wife, Sarah, called to let me know what had happened. I've also spent time with her the last two days, took some vacation time I had coming. I've actually known her even longer than I did Bill." Danny didn't think that it was worth adding that Sarah and he had dated and been lovers for a time. Although he knew Jack O'Malley would have understood that one, too.

"And what can the bishop and I do for you this fine spring day?"

Danny proceeded to tell him about his discomfort with the manner and means of Bill's death, about Bill's concerns that there were those who would be unhappy to an extreme about his planned release of the news of his discovery of the papyrus, and about the ransacking of Bill's study at home by a figure in black, who may have been wearing a priest's collar with his black shirt.

"I trust you enough, Jack, to ask, could there be a person or persons within your communion who you think could go so far as to break into Bill's rectory and steal that fragment of papyrus?"

"And be so desperate as to want to murder Bill in the process?" Jack O'Malley always had a way of getting right to the point, however uncomfortable it may be.

"Well, yes. I know, it sounds fantastic, but in addition to suspicions I have about the means of Bill's death, I cannot bring myself to believe that Bill Brand would commit suicide. It just doesn't add up. Now, I know, the death and the break-in may not actually have any connection, but maybe we should accept that there really is no such thing as 'coincidence.'"

The monsignor leaned back in his chair and paused a moment. Then he leaned forward again and adopted a much more serious aspect.

"Neither do I understand why Bill would indulge in the sin of suicide, but everyone from the news media to you yourself,

Danny, have said that the police investigated and found no evidence, no suspect, no one's motive, no basis to call it anything other than suicide."

Jack O'Malley's demeanor relaxed again and he kiddingly chided Danny a little bit. "You haven't been reading those novels or watching those movies again, have you Danny? You know, the ones with Opus Dei assassins going around trying to keep the truth about Jesus and Mary Magdalene from being revealed? That the Roman Catholic Church, the Vatican, His Holiness, and all the cardinals and bishops fear a total collapse of the Faith as a result of a dubious scrap of first-century papyrus?" He laughed robustly once again.

"Well, no," Danny replied, feeling just a bit embarrassed. "But you and I know that in any religion, any group, any community, there are occasional individuals who become so extreme in their beliefs and views, so detached from reality and good sense, so zealous to the extreme, that they will commit violent acts like murder. Is there anyone like that among the 215 parishes of your diocese?"

"Father John in McKees Rocks does come to mind," Jack admitted. "A very serious young man, involved in Restoring Creation, the environmental action people, drives a green Prius as a symbol of how 'green' his commitment is. He considers himself a true defender of the Faith. He's so devout that every Lenten season he does a complete fast, nothing but liquids for forty days. Says he wants to resist the devil like Christ did in his forty days and nights of temptation by Satan in the gospel accounts. Gets so goofy sometimes that he has to be taken to the emergency room," Jack roared.

Danny had to laugh, too....not that he would make light of anyone's spiritual discipline. "But seriously, no radical priest you can think of who might possibly turn to violence if his beliefs were challenged?"

"No, here at the diocese we would act if one of our priests got so extreme as to go that far. We would want to handle it before any civil authorities got involved."

Danny knew that was true. The Church in Rome

considered itself the highest authority in the Christian Faith, in the entire world, actually, Christ's representatives on Earth, with the Pope as the sole Vicar of Christ. Of course, the diocese deciding to act in regard to a priest who gave them concern often amounted to little more than transferring him somewhere far away from where he had been previously assigned, but Danny was not so indiscreet as to comment on that to the monsignor.

Monsignor O'Malley leaned forward and spoke more softly, as if someone might overhear him. "Let's face it, Danny. It doesn't matter to us what ancient textual discovery is proclaimed. When Bill's papyrus would get media attention, no matter how many respected scholars might back it, the diocese, the Vatican, our entire official apparatus would denounce the whole matter as unauthentic and heretical at best,a complete hoax and fraud at the worst."

Jack went on, "We have always maintained the authority to tell our faithful what is Holy Scripture, how they are to understand it and apply it to their lives. We tell them what to believe, what is true and Christian, and they believe it. Why else would so many of our believers around the world continue to produce as many children as possible, even when birth control and smaller families would enable so many of them to have more comfortable and prosperous lives? We unvaryingly tell them that it is God's will for them to reproduce. Bill Brand's papyrus didn't need to be stolen. And, he certainly didn't need to be murdered by any nefarious Catholic radical priest. It would be swept aside easily and become just another would-be scandal of the day, gone tomorrow at the latest."

Danny knew that he wasn't being condescending and overly-dismissive. Jack O'Malley was merely speaking the fact of the matter. The Roman Church would smoothly handle the matter and go on as if it didn't mean anything. Which to them, it wouldn't. He thanked the monsignor for his time, his frankness, and his friendship. O'Malley, in turn, put a big, affectionate arm around Danny's shoulders and told him not to wait so long to come back.

"And the diocese will be represented at Bill's funeral Friday morning. I can't be there myself," said O'Malley; "have to go down to one of our parishes and regretfully close their struggling school, but Mrs. Brand, the congregation, and the neighborhood of Shadyside will receive the consolation and prayers of our delegation. I think I can have the auxiliary bishop attend. The Episcopal diocese might like him to have a guest part."

And of course, the news media will notice them, thought Danny. He paused at the receptionist's door as Monsignor O'Malley headed back to his office. When Jack was out of sight, Danny asked the receptionist, "Say, could you spare a diocesan directory? Mine is old and out of date."

"Of course," the young woman said cheerfully. "Here you are," and handed it to him.

Danny thanked her and left with a friendly wave. Back in his Jeep, he sat and thumbed through the directory. There. Father John Anderson, Church of the Blessed Sacrament, Carson Street, McKees Rocks. He'd grab some lunch in Oakland and think about his meeting with Jack O'Malley. Jack's was a long-standing friendship, but Danny had not been entirely convinced by the way Jack had handled him, and he had no illusions about where the monsignor's deepest loyalties lay.

CHAPTER TWENTY-ONE

Danny was unsure if he should try to find out more about Father John or not. He decided to go to an old, favorite diner near the Pitt campus and grab a sandwich and Coke like he had so often during his student days to consider what to do next.

Sarah was spending the day finalizing funeral arrangements with Sally and Ken at the church. She also had to meet with the florist, the caterer and the ladies of the church for the lunch after the interment. Her attention was also needed at the mortuary, and she had to refine the half-page with photo for obituary for The Pittsburgh Post Gazette. And, of course she would have to talk to a dizzying number of people eager to express their condolences. At Sarah's insistence, Danny agreed to join them for a light supper at the rectory.

As he parked the Grand Cherokee down the street from Len's Diner, he noticed a lime green Prius several cars behind him pulling into another space. The driver bent over quickly as if to look into the glove compartment, but it looked to Danny as if he was dressed in black. Danny shook his head and mentally scolded himself. He was working himself into paranoia. He had to stop, calm down, and sort things through.

As was always the case, the diner was bustling with students, faculty members, and various others having lunch in what had been a fast-food place long before the modern fast-food chains became a way of life for Americans. Len had perfected the process of taking the order fast, cooking hot meals fast with a team of skilled cooks working the grills and fry baskets, serving the customers fast with their checks accompanying their orders, taking the money fast, and moving them out fast to make space for the waiting next customer. It was the proverbial well-oiled, or well-greased, as the case may be, restaurant machine.

Len's son, Lenny Jr., now ran the fast-paced operation, but he paused for a moment when he saw Danny in line.

"Dr. Henriks, long time no see. Welcome back. Jenny, quick take his order."

It was a genuinely warm greeting, but Lenny Jr. never broke stride and the machine kept whirring as customer turn-over never came to a stop. Danny's order appeared practically as soon as he had settled on his stool at the counter, slipped his jacket off, and looked up again.

Len's was not exactly the place to lean back and contemplate the circumstances of Bill's death, but he couldn't help but glance at the clientele coming and going to see if a fellow in priest's garb and collar had come in after him and merged into the crowd. He mentally checked off items as he munched on his sandwich and sipped his Coke. Fast, of course.

He hadn't learned anything from his phone call to the Keystone range house. If Bill had altered his habits with choke tubes in his shotguns, Steve the range master hadn't noticed. Maybe Danny could check with the range master or others at the Cedar Club up in Northern Michigan.

Somewhere out there was the man who had ransacked Bill's study at home. The papyrus fragment was missing, presumably taken by the mysterious, perhaps priestly, burglar. Jack O'Malley had been of no help except to mention a rather kooky young priest who was something of an environmental activist and considered himself a self-appointed defender of Catholic orthodoxy and the pure faith of Christendom. Oh, and he drove an environmentally-friendly, light green Prius, perhaps like the one that took off from the curb near the rectory last night, or the one that pulled in several spots behind Danny's Grand Cherokee near Len's just now.

He dutifully took his quickly-provided check and paid for

his fast lunch, rising in the same motion to make room for the next customer standing close behind him. All the while thinking about his check list for the day. He admitted that, in reality, he had little more than the constant feeling that none of it made sense. Like his initial glimpse of the little piece of Tiny's friendship bracelet on Bill's study floor at the church, it just wasn't right. Bottom line, he couldn't conceive of Bill committing suicide. Not ever. And certainly not now.

He got back in his Jeep and couldn't keep from looking back for the green Prius. It was there, driving away and heading west.

Probably nothing, Danny thought. But, with no plans for the afternoon, and not seeing Sarah again until evening, it wouldn't hurt to make a little drive west himself, go past downtown Pittsburgh and across the I-376 Bridge, west on Highway 51, and stop by Church of the Blessed Sacrament. Maybe Father John would be in the office and be willing to answer a few questions.

CHAPTER TWENTY-TWO

The Parish Office of Blessed Sacrament was on a side street, and Danny found a parking space just down the block and went in the office. The church secretary was back from her own lunch break and looked up from her desk as if surprised that anyone would be coming in.

"May I help you? Are you looking for someone?"

"My name is the Rev. Dr. Daniel Henriks. I'm the pastor at South Presbyterian. Would Father John Anderson be in this afternoon?"

"Yes, the Father is in the sacristy. If you don't mind having a seat, Reverend, I'll go find him for you."

Danny obediently sat and waited. Before long the secretary returned with Father John in tow. He was tall, a bit over six feet. He wore the standard black priest's garb with white clerical collar, sported a rather scraggly reddish beard, and a particularly intense look behind his wire-rimmed glasses.

"Dr. Henriks, I understand. And what brings you out to Blessed Sacrament this afternoon? How may I be of help?"

"Thank you for seeing me, Father Anderson. Is there somewhere we can talk in private?"

"Okay. Follow me into my office," Father John replied, shutting the door between his office and the secretary's after them. He motioned for Danny to sit in front of his desk.

"So what brings you here?"

"I was visiting with Monsignor O'Malley just this morning, and he mentioned you to me," Danny answered. Stretching the truth just a bit, he added, "The monsignor thought you might be able to answer some questions I have."

"Why would the pompous, old windbag refer you to me? What questions?"

"Have you heard about the death of Dr. Bill Brand Easter Sunday morning in his study at Church of the Resurrection?"

"Sure, who hasn't? It's been all over the news. They say the old enemy of the environment committed suicide. What of it?"

Danny knew that Father John was referring to the fact that in addition to some of Bill's church members hoping to profit from redevelopment of the Hill those years before, Bill also supported them in their industrial businesses, most of which were not so environmentally friendly. He let it pass, however, and went on.

"Well, the fact is that Dr. Brand's home was also burglarized just last night. An ancient papyrus he stored there has disappeared, apparently taken by the burglar. The intruder was seen driving away in a light green subcompact. The monsignor shared with me that you would have reason to be very upset about the text of the papyrus, that you would consider it to be damaging to Christian orthodoxy, to true faith in Christ, and, oh, you drive a green Prius."

"Now hold on there. Lots of people drive a Prius. Who knows how many of them are colored green in the Greater Pittsburgh area? And I certainly wasn't in Shadyside last night, nor did I have anything to do with this burglary of the Brands' house. Oh, it figures that Jack O'Malley would point a finger at me, the conniving old S.O.B. He's the master of manipulation and deflection, always the devious politician."

"Why would he want to point at you?" Danny asked.

"Well, for one thing, I don't kowtow to him. He considers me an embarrassment to the diocese because I stand up for the True Faith and a Pure Church, without all the hypocrisy and the sacrifice of the poor and needy for the wealth of the church bureaucracy. I organize with others to care for Planet Earth and restore Creation from its poisoning by those who don't care, and I don't mind the fact that the big donors the bishop and the monsignor are so afraid of offending are called to account."

"What about Bill Brand's papyrus?" Danny pressed him. "Would you want to be rid of any challenge it might present to Catholic orthodoxy?"

"Oh, I had heard about it. How it supposedly says something about the relationship of Mary Magdalene to our Lord Jesus, but I certainly haven't seen either the text itself or any photo of it. In any case, there are lots of heretical and apocryphal old manuscripts around the world that exist outside the sacred canon of God's Word. Whatever this one claims, it's just one more, old document of spurious authorship. O'Malley would be much more riled up about it than I."

"How so? He seemed pretty unconcerned this morning when I talked to him."

"Of course, that's his public persona. But the bishop, he, the Vatican, right up to his Holiness the Pope, they're all running scared from all the scandals that have been going on for years now."

"You mean about the Vatican bank, the controversies in the behavior of certain priests, the official cover-ups that people see through more and more?"

"Exactly," Father John said. "And while they make light of the novels and movies and fringe groups that try to make a case for a different understanding of Christ Jesus, it bothers the hell out of them that people pay attention to those things, that some start believing such heresies, and who knows how many previously loyal parishioners drift away from the True Church. You see, Dr. Henriks, not only do the spiritually weak and nominal members go, they take their dollars with them."

"And that doesn't bother you and your associates or friends?"

"Not enough to want Dr. Brand dead, or to try to steal or destroy his dubious bit of papyrus. Someone like Jack O'Malley and his henchmen would be better suspects for you to look into. Believe me, they would not want to have to field even more controversy and dissension, even if they try to dismiss the matter as of no importance. I'd go back to him and put the screws to him more sharply. Of course, I'd do that about anything," Father John finally indulged in a bit of a smile and a chuckle.

"And you're sure that you and your green Prius weren't in Shadyside last night? There's someone who would vouch for you on that?" Danny pressed him.

The hint of a smile disappeared as quickly as it had formed. Father John rose from his chair on the other side of the desk.

"I'm not going to dignify that with a response," he said. "I haven't minded having you here, asking your questions, and I am sorry about the death of your friend, but I've already told you I wasn't there. I may not have a big and prosperous parish, and never will with the likes of the bishop and O'Malley, but I have my integrity and my honesty. You'll have to leave with that. Now I must get on with today's schedule."

"I apologize for offending you," Danny said. "Thank you for your time and your frankness. I'll see myself out."

And he did, but he passed Father John's lime-green Prius parked in the alley behind the church, and he wondered just who it was he could believe. What Father John had told him had a ring of truth about it, but on the other hand, he had just met the man for the first time, and he really didn't know what truly lay in his mind and heart. He had known Jack O'Malley for a lot of years, spent time with him on numerous occasions, and while he had to admit that the monsignor was a shrewd politician and adept at handling people and situations, Danny considered his friendship to be genuine.

As he drove back south and east toward downtown Pittsburgh, questions filled his mind.

Which one, Monsignor O'Malley or Father John, was the truly artful deflector, trying to cast aspersions on the other?

Which one could he really believe?

Did either one have anything at all to do with Bill's demise and/or the disappearance of the papyrus?

There was certainly the matter of the green Prius, but Father John was right, it could have been someone else's. They had no license number or distinguishing features or marks. But there was also the undeniable possibility that it could have been his.

It was an interesting experience, meeting Father John, but Danny didn't feel any closer to knowing just what was going on, other than his perpetual feeling that the whole matter just wasn't right, and that Bill couldn't have taken his own life. He mulled and stewed all the way back to his South Hills home.

It was late afternoon when he finally got there. End of the business day traffic had slowed his return, but he had an hour or more to sit and think before going to Sarah's again that evening. Surely the police would have told her something about their investigation of the burglary. He also considered that maybe he should face up to the official finding of suicide and quit tormenting her with his fruitless queries. Normally confident about his keen judgment, the Rev. Dr. Henriks vacillated between feeling determined to push on until every little doubt was satisfied and feeling as though he was just making problems for an old friend when she should be allowed to mourn and find some genuine closure.

It was definitely time to slide into the Adirondack chair and mellow out with some Crown Royal Black before going to the rectory for supper.

CHAPTER TWENTY-THREE

After finishing a slow-cooked, pepper-crusted, beef pot roast with fresh vegetables, Danny's spring favorite, rhubarb pie, and lots of dark roast coffee, Danny, Sarah, Ken, and Sally sat at the magnificent Stickley oak table in the rectory's formal dining room. They relaxed with one of Bill's favorites, Bristol Cream Sherry, and caught up on their respective activities on a busy Wednesday.

"Sally, that was a truly great meal, and not exactly what I think of as a 'light supper'," said Danny. "Being single and living alone, I tend to eat out a lot, not wanting to cook sometimes for just me, so I really appreciate being here for this feast, especially with the three of you."

Sarah added, "Sally's been a godsend in all this nightmare. I'm thinking about keeping her on." All four laughed. "And Ken, my always-protective older brother. He's tackled the long list of things to do with his usual energy and devotion to taking care of his little sister. And Danny, you're my oldest friend, and have always been there for me. The last few days have been heartbreaking, confusing, frightening, but I've had you to lean on. Bill would be grateful to his longtime best friend."

"A toast to all of us!" shouted Ken, and they clinked glasses and each took a sip of the sweet sherry. Frankly, they needed some lightening up on the dark events of the last four days.

"So, Ken," asked Danny, "Sarah said that your wife, two

children and their spouses, and five grandchildren are all coming in on flights tomorrow for the Friday funeral?"

"Yes, we're grateful that they could all take time off and be here. And the airline has been really great about booking seats for them on bereavement status. The George Bush Intercontinental Airport in Houston is so big and busy that they have to be there early tomorrow morning for all the preflight stuff. It'll be a fast trip, I'm afraid. We have to fly out again Friday night."

Sally jumped in, "And my husband, Ronald, and I have no children or grandchildren, so it's just the two of us. He's been traveling for work, but he'll be here tomorrow, also."

"That's why she works so hard at mothering me," Sarah laughed. "And I'm so high maintenance and demanding that it's like having five kids of her own."

"Go on," Sally protested. "I'm just glad we live so close so that I can pitch in and help in a time like this. Not that we've....ever had a time like...." Her voice caught and a tear reemerged.

The lighter mood temporarily darkened, Sally put her wine glass down, rallied, and said, "I'll take the dishes out to the kitchen." To which Ken added, "And I'll help you."

Sarah suggested to Danny that the two of them step out to the enclosed sun room off the dining room. The bright, spring sun was going down, and they looked out together to the setting sun.

Sarah took his arm, looked up at him, and said, "Ken and his family will fly back to Houston Friday evening after the funeral and interment. I insisted that Sally take a break from me and all this and go home for the weekend." Sarah paused before continuing.

"I told them both that I was going to head up to the cottage in Leelanau Saturday morning. I need to get away and I need to look around up there, try to decide what to do with Bill's shooting things and other outdoor stuff there. I may even think about whether it makes sense to list it for sale. It was always his place most of all. Would you consider going with me? It would be a big help to have some muscle."

Her smile at this was radiant, but Danny read nothing into

it, just that he wanted to continue to be there for her, to help if he could. And while he had never been at the Brand cottage, he had visited the Traverse City, Michigan, area before and liked being there.

"Okay, if you're sure you want me to. I don't have to be back at the church until next Tuesday morning. It's about a twelve-hour drive. If we leave early Saturday morning, assuming you feel up to it after Friday, we could be there by suppertime. We could go to Amical in Traverse City for supper. We wouldn't have to leave there to come back to Pittsburgh until sometime Monday morning. That would leave Saturday evening and all day Sunday to go through stuff, think about what you want to do, maybe even meet with a realtor Monday morning before heading south. If that's what you decide to do."

"Sounds perfect," she beamed.

Danny added, "I'll call right away and see if I can book the Leelanau Bed & Breakfast for myself for Saturday night and Sunday night. They should have an opening this early in the season. It will also give me an opportunity to swing by the Cedar Rod & Gun Club during Sunday shooting and talk to the range master there about Bill's handling of his shotgun before a round of trap."

Sarah nodded, smiled, and seemed more relaxed as she sipped her sherry.

CHAPTER TWENTY-FOUR

Sally and Ken joined them in the sun room with their wine glasses, and they attempted to relax from all the stress.

Danny finally couldn't help himself and asked the three siblings, "Have you heard anything from the police yet about last night's break-in and ransacking of Bill's study here in the rectory?"

"They seemed to do a very thorough investigation while they were here," Ken replied. "They dusted for prints in the office and surrounding areas of the house. They were outside, checking for footprints left in the dirt, especially under the shrubbery he had run into over by the sidewalk. They seemed most professional, but dang, I wish I had my friend from the Texas Rangers here. Now *they* know how to track a man down."

Sarah said, "Your friend Sergeant Bradley, the detective, was kind enough to call me on my cell phone, however, to say that at this point it seems likely that the burglar wore gloves and shoes with little tread on the soles. They're still analyzing, but may not turn up any prints that would help connect to a possible suspect."

"They also canvassed the neighborhood," Ken added, "and while no one saw anyone go into or out of the house, Mrs. Lamont across and down the street reported seeing an unfamiliar, green subcompact car parked along the curb about that time. Sergeant Bradley said she only mentioned it because she had never seen it there before, and wondered who it might be. He suggested that we keep our eyes open in case it comes by again."

Sally chimed in, too, "And I have a pad and pen handy in

case we can get a license number. Can't rely upon my memory for more than a second or two, I'm afraid."

Danny decided that Thursday morning would be a good time to give Jim Bradley a call again. Or he might go back over to the precinct and tell him in detail about his visit with both Monsignor O'Malley and Father John. He could suggest that the police look into Father John's history a bit, point out that he drove a lime green Prius, and about the sighting of the green Prius near Len's. Who knows, maybe someone didn't like the fact that he kept nosing around about Bill's death and the missing papyrus.

Sarah told Danny that she would fill in Sally and Ken later about their decision to go up to Leelanau about the cottage. As she walked him to the door, she again embraced and kissed him.

"It was a good time tonight. I'm glad we could all be together."

"It was. Your brother and sister are good people. Oh, and since they'll be gone after the funeral and my friend Tiny knows the layout from being here, is it okay with you if I ask him to swing by and check on the rectory Saturday through Monday, maybe keep an eye out for the green Prius? Besides, not only does he have a business of providing 'protective services,' but he really feels like he owes us after yesterday."

Sarah agreed wholeheartedly. "Tell Tiny I'd be grateful for his help, and no hard feelings about the rough handling yesterday outside his office."

As he opened the door to leave, Danny shared that he was going to fill Jim Bradley in on what O'Malley said about Father John and his green Prius, and about the car that might have been following him in Oakland. He decided not to mention his meeting with Father John in McKees Rocks. He didn't want Sarah to think that he was obsessing so much that he was getting overly-involved in his paranoia.

"Good night, Sarah, I'll call tomorrow, promise."

"Good night, Daniel, and please be careful."

He was, all the way home. He locked up and rechecked the doors and windows once he got there. Danny Henriks, always self-confident, for the first time in a long time felt a nagging anxiety.

Who was out there, and didn't want him snooping around, asking questions? If it turned out that it wasn't this kooky Father John, or someone acting in cahoots with Jack O'Malley, who else could it be? He could always hope that Bradley and his detective squad had developed some leads. He'd have to sleep on it and find out tomorrow morning.

CHAPTER TWENTY-FIVE

Thursday morning found Danny on the phone again to the precinct office of Sergeant Jim Bradley. Despite wondering if he was becoming a nuisance and hindrance, he was told that Sergeant Bradley would indeed be glad to have him stop in. So he drove there, grabbing a fast food breakfast sandwich and cup of coffee on the way. As a Pittsburgh City Police Chaplain, volunteer and part-time, of course, he was always welcome to take advantage of the coffee at the station, but frankly almost anything was better than that, at least to Danny's tastebuds.

Jim was meeting with a couple of his detectives when Danny arrived, but that was over soon, and he stuck his head out of the door of his office and called for Danny to come on in.

"We're going to have to give you your own office if you're in here every day," Jim kidded him. Danny took it as good-natured, but maybe that he was being a bother.

"You're going to have to make better coffee for that to happen," Danny ribbed him back, holding up his to-go cup for display. "I just thought I better tell you some of what's happened with me the last couple of days."

He proceeded to tell him what Monsignor O'Malley had said about Father John and his green Prius, about the green Prius that may have followed him yesterday in Oakland and parked behind him at Len's, about his subsequent meeting with Father John himself at Blessed Sacrament Church, and that he had heard about the green sub-compact parked near the Church of the

Resurrection campus around the time of Tuesday night's break-in and burglary at the rectory.

Jim Bradley listened carefully and patiently, jotted down a few notes, and said in reply, "Dr. Henriks, I appreciate you sharing this with me. My guys can do a little inquiry about this Father John, but I'm afraid, Chaplain, the problem is, we don't really have much to go on. There were no fingerprints. The burglar certainly wore gloves. The footprints outside were indistinct, except for approximate size. There was no other trace evidence like fibers foreign to the household or anything the guy might have dropped. We have no license plate number or distinguishing features on the green subcompact seen nearby. Although it is true that none of the neighbors questioned could account for the car. But still, there's an overwhelming number of green subcompact cars in the Greater Pittsburgh area, to say nothing of beyond."

"We're running through the usual suspects. The B & E guys, burglars and their fences. But we just don't have the personnel to spend a lot of time and effort when there's so little to work with. That ancient papyrus described seems to have been the only thing taken, according to Mrs. Brand. Nothing else of any value seems to be missing, so we have that to go on, has to be a pretty limited market for something like that. But we don't have any idea whether it might have been stolen for possible sale, or for some other reason, so no clear motive that could possibly point to one or more suspects."

Danny had to agree with everything Jim Bradley was telling him. Jim had proven over and over in his profession that he was one of the best investigators around, but it was hard to investigate without evidence or facts. And what he had told Jim about the green Prius car or cars offered next to nothing. He thanked the sergeant for his time and patience, for all the effort his men were making, and then remembered that he had written authorization from Sarah to pick up the shotgun.

"Here's a note from Mrs. Brand to receive the shotgun, Jim. Where do I get it?"

Sergeant Bradley looked at the signed note and said, "This is all I need. The sergeant down in the Evidence Locker has the gun. I'll send a uniform down to get it for you."

As the two of them walked toward the main entrance, the uniformed officer returned promptly with Bill's shotgun. Danny signed a form for it, shook Jim's hand and thanked him yet again. He glanced at the muzzle, and noted that the choke tube was still in place. His experienced eye, however, also caught the fact that the tube was not screwed in quite all the way. Just about a thread was slightly exposed. Bill Brand would never, ever, be that sloppy about putting in a choke tube. Not that it was something Danny could prove. It could always be contended that in his depressed state Bill had not practiced his customary exactness. But Danny was quietly more convinced that someone else had to have handled the gun early Easter morning. And they used it to murder Bill.

Bradley concluded with, "We'll see if this Father John character has any history of illegal activity. But it'll take more than being boisterous at a Greenpeace rally. Okay, Chaplain? Oh, and you really should leave the investigating up to us, you know."

"I know you're doing everything you can, Sergeant. Thanks again. And I apologize if I stuck my nose in too much. I'll try to stick to official prayers, spiritual and counseling support, and invocations at banquets so far as the police are concerned. I'll even drink some of your precinct coffee without complaining. Some of the time."

They both laughed at that and Danny left the station. He placed the gun, slipped into a light, temporary cloth case, in the back of his Jeep. As he drove away, Danny admitted to himself that he had been meddling in official police business. They really were much more skilled and better equipped to pursue the matter of the break-in.

Besides, Jack O'Malley hadn't really pointed at the priest as a possible suspect in the burglary, much less so as someone who could have anything to do with Bill's death. Only that he was an activist priest who was particularly zealous about his Catholic faith and calling. Or could he have been deflecting inquiry away from himself and his cohorts as Father John suggested?

He took out his cell phone and called Tiny's number. It

went straight to voicemail, "Hey, dude, don't be rude; leave your number, I'll call you back."

He knew that Sarah, Ken and Sally were occupied this morning with final things before the big funeral tomorrow morning. Danny decided that maybe there was nothing else he could do at this point and that he himself should take a break from his amateur detective messing around and go home and work on his eulogy for Bill at the reception after the funeral.

Danny decided that it wouldn't hurt to swing by Shadyside, stop at the rectory, and at least see how the three of them were doing. Ken's family wasn't arriving from Houston until close to suppertime, so he was sure that the three would be at Sarah's and the church, to get as much done as possible before going to the airport to meet them.

Besides, maybe he could mooch a sandwich. It was getting close to lunchtime. Knowing the drill, he also figured that by now they would be buried in goodies brought over by the ladies of the church. Mourning food. Probably casseroles, too. Yes, checking in at the rectory sounded like the thing to do.

CHAPTER TWENTY-SIX

Danny pulled into the Church of the Resurrection parking lot and passed two florists' delivery trucks unloading massive arrangements of flowers through the side door of the church. He knew that many more would be rushing in Friday morning before the service, and that even now Margaret was probably away from the Secretary's Office, herding the florists around the sanctuary, making sure the tripods and baskets were placed properly. He parked at the far end, near to the rectory. And doggone it, he could have sworn he saw a green subcompact disappearing down the street past the front of the house.

Danny was right. By the time he knocked on the door, Ken, Sally and Sarah were gathered in the kitchen, deciding what casserole dish and luscious dessert should be selected for their lunch.

"Have enough for an itinerant preaching man?"

"Enough?" Sally quipped back, "We'll be able to feed the whole congregation for a week at least." True to her nature, she was taking charge of both dealing with the food that threatened to fill the kitchen, and fixing their lunch.

"Pull up a chair," Ken said. "Join us."

Sarah went to him and gave him a hug and a light kiss on his cheek. "I'm glad you surprised us. How was your morning?"

As they dug into plates of the classic but delicious tuna casserole, to be followed by his rhubarb pie, Danny told them about his visit once again to the precinct and his not-very-encouraging conversation with Sergeant Bradley.

"The police really don't think they have much to investigate with concerning the break-in. But we did bring up the sightings of that little green car, probably a Prius." Danny paused with a thoughtful look in his eye. "And, you know, I could swear I saw one just now as I pulled up to park, driving by on the street in front of the rectory."

"Oh, dear," said Sally, "Do you suppose he's come back to scout us for another robbery attempt? Maybe you interrupted him before he was finished robbing your home, Sarah."

"I think that's highly unlikely," Sarah replied. "As Sergeant Bradley said, there are lots of green subcompact cars in the Pittsburgh area. It's probably just coincidental."

Well, I still don't believe in coincidences, thought Danny. But he admitted to himself that he might be foolish for fixating on the matter of this green Prius.

"So," Ken asked, "they're not getting very far with the burglary investigation. What a shame that this has intervened to distract from Bill's suicide and funeral."

As soon as he mentioned it, he wished he had simply said "Bill's death." The idea of suicide, so inexplicable, was extremely upsetting to them all.

But Sarah didn't seem bothered by his words. "Come on now, let's enjoy this pie. I know Daniel will have a big slice of rhubarb, but there's also blueberry and apple, and I think you said banana cream, Sally?"

"And Boston cream, too," Sally added. "Like I said, we can feed the whole church."

"Not with my rhubarb," Danny protested. And the death and the break-in were dropped for the time being, at least from the conversation, but vexingly, never from Danny's mind. When lunch was over, while Sally and Ken were clearing the table and loading the dishwasher, Danny mentioned the shotgun to Sarah.

"I picked up Bill's shotgun from the police station with the note you signed, authorizing me to do so. It's in the back of my Jeep."

Sarah wrinkled her face with obvious disgust.

"Well, I don't want it; I don't want to see it ever again. You can keep it for all I care."

"How 'bout I take it down in the basement and put it back in Bill's gun safe? It'll be out of sight there and kept safe. The police didn't seem to need it anymore, having decided that it confirmed an act of suicide, but maybe you should keep it here, just in case."

"In case of what?" Sarah asked. "It's of no use to anyone. I wish it was just destroyed."

"I'm sorry, Sarah, but the more I see it and think of it, I really don't think that Bill used it on himself. And even if the police have concluded that he did, at the least, someone else handled that gun before it killed Bill."

Sarah shuddered and pulled away from him. But Danny repeated himself.

"I truly am sorry. I wish I didn't feel this way, but the gun just isn't right; it isn't the way Bill did things."

He knew full well that Sarah disliked guns and especially that Bill owned and used them. He had obviously upset her, but Danny couldn't help it, he had to go with what he truly believed. And for the umpteenth time, he didn't believe that his best friend had taken his own life. Someone had murdered him in his own church. But maybe he should let it rest for now with Sarah and go.

CHAPTER TWENTY-SEVEN

Sarah gave him the combination to the gun safe. Danny went down and placed the shotgun in it; he locked the safe again, and went back up to leave. Danny and Sarah agreed at the door that he would spend the rest of the afternoon at his home, preparing his eulogy, and she would get back to the final touches with Sally and Ken for Friday.

The ladies of the church were taking charge in their usual manner of the post-funeral, post-interment, early afternoon lunch reception in the church Fellowship Hall, but they still wanted Sarah to come over so they could ask her what she wanted about this and that. How many floral arrangements should be brought down from the sanctuary to put around the hall, and should there be one on a head table? Should there be a head table at all? There would be a lot of official people and dignitaries. Or did Sarah want just a round table for herself and her family like all the others, so she could more easily get up and circulate around to the others attending? There was a myriad of such details to decide, none of them little as far as the church women were concerned.

Things like that would fill up Sarah's afternoon, but she had insisted that by late afternoon she would be free to go to the airport to greet and pick up Ken's family. She knew her way around there, where to park and where to go, much better than Ken or Sally. As usual, there was no arguing with her. She promised them and Danny that she would find time to rest that evening, if that was really possible with ten more family members arriving and all that catching up to do.

Danny returned home, heated up a cup of coffee, and sat at his desk to think and write. There was such a tremendous volume of attributes, accomplishments, and fond personal memories to share about Bill Brand that he had to think hard about what to include and what had to be left out for the sake of time restrictions. Five minutes maximum was what he would shoot for and that much might be pushing the limit, considering all of the other participants who would be getting up to do some part. It was a dangerous thing to attend any event filled with participating clergy. They could be even more compulsive than Danny about getting their own preaching in, whether they had responsibility for the message or not.

The eulogy would actually take place at the reception in the Fellowship Hall, since the traditional death rites in the Episcopal churches did not allow it in the funeral service itself. Bill had been somewhat more relaxed about his services than the Book of Common Worship specified, but since his Assistant Rector Frank would be acting as the host pastor, and since so many Episcopal brass would be in attendance and participating in the service, Frank would be sure to go by the book.

The casket containing the body would be brought to the church by the mortuary hearse thirty minutes before the service. No sooner. No later. It would be wheeled with clergy procession into the church and down the stone floor of the center aisle. The death liturgy would be as the book declared "an Easter liturgy," and befitting the traditional Anglican architecture and adornment of the church and its sanctuary, Rite One in the old, Elizabethan language would be used. The most formal vestments, dominated by white as the color for Easter, but with lots of gold and embroidery, would be worn by the participating priests. There would be lots of candles and banks of floral arrangements on either side of the stone steps leading up to the chancel. Some Episcopal churches put strict limits on the quantity of flowers to adorn the sanctuary for a funeral service, but Church of the Resurrection would go all out for their beloved, esteemed late Rector.

As Danny was envisioning all of the elaborate details that would go into tomorrow's funeral and especially what he would say about Bill in his eulogy at the reception luncheon, his cell rang. It was Tiny, finally getting back to him.

"Hey, Danny, Tiny here. Sorry I didn't see your call this morning. The boys and I had to make our rounds for monthly contributions from the shopkeepers who are grateful for our protection services. Tell me what I can do for you, and it'll be done."

"Well, actually I do have a request for you, Tiny. It would be a big favor."

Danny went on to fill Tiny in on the events of the last couple of days. He also informed Tiny about the plan to go with Sarah to the Brand lake cottage in Leelanau County, Michigan on Saturday morning.

"The police are still investigating the burglary," Danny added, "and they will have normal patrols go by the rectory, but they probably won't even stop there unless they just happen to observe suspicious activity around or in the house, since no one will be there over the weekend. If it's at all possible that that green Prius is hanging around for some reason, it'd be great if you and your protective services could keep your own watch, maybe get a license number or some description of the driver, anything, if it shows up again. Maybe check a couple of times on Saturday, Sunday, and Monday?"

"You got it, Danny. We'll do it on the down-low, real quiet. The good folks of Shadyside might get a little antsy if they see three black brothers hanging around that fancy church and neighborhood."

"Now frankly, Tiny, I don't see why the burglar would try to get into the house again, since he may already have what he wanted. But one theory is that when we heard him in the home study Tuesday night, we may have interrupted the robbery, and that he could return if he doesn't have all that he was after, especially if he observes that no one's home. It would be just a precaution. Probably nothing to it."

"No problem," Tiny assured. "We'll be your own

Neighborhood Watch," he roared in delight with his own joke. "When will the two of you be back?"

"We'll leave up there sometime Monday morning. Probably be back here late that night. I need to be in my church office Tuesday morning, and Mrs. Brand said that she wants to get back to deal with a lot on her plate after Dr. Brand's funeral. She needs to return to the mortuary, meet with their attorney about the estate and any death taxes, probably go back to the cemetery, do something with all his clothes and personal stuff. It's pretty overwhelming."

"Yah, I remember my Nana's funeral. The wake alone went on for days. A lot longer for all the other things. Say, how's your head feeling? We're really sorry about that."

"A lot better," Danny chuckled. "But the bump is still there, and still hurts, too. But, tell your boys no hard feelings. All is forgiven. Oh, and cell phone reception is great up there in Leelanau, including on Grand Traverse Bay where the Brand cottage is located, so in case you need to call me, just use my cell number."

"You can count on it. Let me know when you get back okay."

They ended their call and Danny resumed writing his eulogy. He decided to stay in for supper and the evening, knowing that Friday would be busy to the extreme. He'd call Sarah early in the evening tonight just to touch base and make sure she was feeling okay. And she still had Ken and Sally with her, as well as all those church ladies in the church, and more relatives about to arrive. If anything, she probably had too many people who would be watching out for her and taking care of her.

CHAPTER TWENTY-EIGHT

Danny arrived at the Church of the Resurrection early on Friday morning. He stopped by the Church Office and saw Father Frank.

"Is there anything I can do to be of assistance?"

"Good morning, Dr. Henriks. No, everything seems to be under control, but thanks for asking."

Margaret dashed through the office and chipped in with, "He doesn't have to deal with these florists. They keep coming like the locusts of the plagues of Egypt. I'll be back in a few," she added for Father Frank's benefit.

Danny knew that part of her assumed duties was making sure that the young assistant rector knew what to do and that he would do it the way it had to be done.

"Do you have just a minute or two, Frank?" asked Danny.

"I guess so, at least until Margaret gets back and resumes giving me directions. You'd think she was the new rector."

"I've known Margaret for years before you came to the church," Danny said. "She's a take-charge kind of person, but she'll also be a tremendous help for you in this difficult time. Don't let her bother you."

"I suppose. But I know I'll be the one leading the parish until the bishop appoints either an interim rector or a permanent replacement for Dr. Brand. I just wish she'd recognize my authority. I know what I'm doing. Well, never mind," Frank shook his head, "What did you want to talk about?"

"I was merely going to suggest that when things start to settle down next week, you might want to check in with Mrs. Brand at the rectory. I know you'll want to give her spiritual support and pastoral care, but a hard fact that she probably hasn't had time to think about, and you probably haven't, either, is that whoever is appointed by the bishop to occupy the Rector's Office and take the pulpit will likely be moving into the rectory, especially if he or she has a family coming with them. Mrs. Brand may have to face the challenge of having to pack and move out sooner rather than later, in addition to having to grieve for her husband."

"Oh, I...yes, that's right, I suppose. I mean, well, I knew that, of course. She'll have plenty of help. But I won't be able to see to it personally. Starting tomorrow I have a week of vacation time scheduled and will be on a trip. A retired priest from the diocese will officiate at Sunday services. But I'll make sure that Mrs. Brand is well taken care of, you don't have to worry about that."

"I appreciate it, Frank, and she will, too. And don't be too bothered by Margaret or by all the demands on you right now. You'll sort it all out, one thing at a time."

Frank squared his shoulders on his bit-over six-foot frame and replied, "As I said, I have it all under control."

Danny wasn't sure about that. Margaret would ride herd on everything at the church, including Frank. He also wasn't sure about Frank's planned vacation trip. A great many ministers and priests understandably schedule spring vacation breaks with their church personnel committees or parish councils after the busy demands of the Lenten/Easter church season. But, the loss of Dr. Brand, especially in such a tragic and horrific way, was devastating to their congregation. The pain and mourning was both widespread and continuing well after the death and the funeral today. As undoubtedly deserved as Frank's week of vacation was, Danny didn't think it was a good idea for Frank to follow through with his plans. The members of the Church of the Resurrection needed to know that their assistant rector was there for them, ministering to them in that time of loss. But it wasn't Danny's responsibility, and it wasn't his decision, so he held his tongue.

Margaret rushed back into the office just then. "There, the

sanctuary has as many floral arrangements as we want. Any more that are delivered last-minute will just have to go into the lounge, or even down to Fellowship Hall. Although I better check the tags. There are a few Mrs. Fuddy-duddies who would throw a fit if *their* arrangement wasn't in the service."

She took a breath and switched gears, "Oh, Frank, the Diocese Office should be open by now. You'd better call and make sure of how many spaces need to be reserved for them in the front pews. The bishop will sit in the chancel, of course, but you better know how many other chairs need to be up there for key liturgists."

She turned and dashed off again.

Danny glanced over toward Frank and saw him roll his eyes upward and shake his head. Somehow, Frank really needed to know that Margaret was one of his greatest assets, not his tormentor. But youth found that hard to learn sometimes. And it really wasn't Danny's business.

He told Frank that he was going to go over to the rectory and see Mrs. Brand, and that he would be back at the church well before the funeral service. He needed to look for Tim to arrive, and he wanted to get a seat in a back pew for the two of them in what would definitely be a packed church, including television and radio reporters setting up outside the main doors and to the sides of the walk. There was no way Margaret would let Frank allow any cameras inside the sanctuary, not even from the back loft. It just wasn't done.

Glancing at his watch, Danny saw that it was going on 9:30. Sarah and Ken and his wife would be up and probably dressed and ready for the 11:00 service. Sally had gone home to Brentwood to get herself ready, and Ronald and she would be arriving at any minute. Other family members had stayed at an area motel last night, but would be gathering at the rectory about 10:00 to organize before walking over to the church. He figured he had about half an hour to beg a cup of coffee and see how Sarah was doing, so he walked over to the house.

CHAPTER TWENTY-NINE

Sarah came to the door to greet Danny with a little hug and a face that looked slightly reddened from recent tears.

"I hope I'm not intruding," Danny said. "I just wanted to check on how you're doing."

"Daniel, come in please. I'm fine. The coffee in the kitchen is hot, and your favorite mug is sitting by the coffee maker. Sit down with us. We have a little time before the others arrive."

Ken was at the breakfast nook table with his wife, both all dressed and ready for the day to start. He got up and strode over to shake Danny's hand.

"Good morning, Dr. Henriks...er, Danny. I want you to meet my wife, Valerie. You'll meet the rest of our tribe in a little bit when they get over here from the motel. I've already called them this morning to make sure they're all rounded up and ready to move out."

Danny reached the table and took Valerie's offered hand.

"It's a pleasure to meet you, although I'm sorry about the circumstances. You have my sincere sympathy about the death of your brother-in-law. I hope your hurried trip went okay."

"Thank you," Valerie replied. "Yes, actually the airline was very helpful and accommodating, and we even arrived on time early last evening. Please pull up a chair and join us."

The four of them sat around the little table with their cups of coffee, and Valerie wasn't shy about continuing the conversation.

"Ken and Sarah have been filling me in with more detail about the bizarre things that have happened this past week. I mean, it was just more horrible than words can express how Bill died, but then to have that break-in here at the house two nights later. Why it's more than a body can bear. Sarah's been lucky to have you for support."

She reached over and patted Danny's arm with a big smile.

"Daniel is my oldest friend," Sarah said. "He was the one I reached out to early Easter Sunday morning when Bill's body was first found by the custodian at the church. He left his church on such a special morning just to come over here for me."

"And he was with you, coming back here to the rectory, when you surprised the burglar. Isn't that what I heard?" Valerie asked.

"Yes, we walked in on him ransacking Bill's study here at home," Danny confirmed. "I just wish I could have caught him, tackled him and held him until the police got here to arrest him."

"Well, I'm glad you didn't," Sarah said. "I mean, you could have gotten yourself hurt. Who knows how dangerous a man like that might be?"

"Which is precisely why I told them I wished my Texas Ranger friend, Al, was here," Ken inserted. "Hon, you've met him. He'd have that coward lassoed and hog-tied in no time."

Sarah changed the subject. "Let's set all that aside for today. Today is for Bill, and we need to focus on honoring him in this service and at the reception."

"Hear, hear," Ken agreed. "It's all about Bill. And you, too, Sarah. We're all here for you. And that even includes all those big-wigs soon to arrive at the church. And didn't you get a phone call just about half an hour ago from the Catholic monsignor himself? Guess a delegation of them will be here, even that assistant bishop, or whatever they call him?"

Danny turned toward Sarah with a questioning look, and she responded to Ken's question.

"That's true; Monsignor O'Malley called to express the personal condolences of both the bishop and himself. He said that he regretted that neither of them could attend due to important commitments on their schedules, but that the auxiliary bishop would be at the service, as well as a couple of other diocesan staff people. The Most Rev. Williams will have a guest part in the service."

"And didn't he also mention something about the break-in?" Ken went on. "I heard you say something on the phone about a paper, parchment, something. It was stolen, I guess."

"Oh, yes, that papyrus that Bill brought back from the Holy Land," Sarah agreed. "I'm surprised he would even mention that tattered, old thing, but he seemed particularly curious about whether it was still missing, whether the police might have any leads on retrieving it. With Bill gone, I certainly don't have any interest in it. Anyway, I told the monsignor that I would have Danny call him or let him know if it turned up."

Danny thought about what Sarah had just said. It struck him as unusual that Jack O'Malley would be so clumsy as to bring up the missing papyrus during a call to express condolences to a grieving widow. He was usually much more smooth and subtle than that.

Was Father John right? Were O'Malley and his Roman Catholic hierarchy more alarmed about the existence of the papyrus than he let on when Danny had met with him? If the monsignor had been involved in the theft of it, or, God forbid, in Bill's death, he surely wouldn't have mentioned the papyrus at all, would he? Unless, again, Father John was correct, that he was trying to deflect any connection with the papyrus away from himself, acting as though he didn't know of its whereabouts. But on the other hand, if he really didn't know where it was, why would he bother bringing it up in such a phone call unless he was genuinely worried about it resurfacing again? Well, there wasn't time and opportunity to get into any of that this morning. It was almost 10:00, so Danny moved to end the discussion.

"Sarah," he said, "the rest of your family will be arriving any minute now; and I should get back to the church. I need to touch base with some people and Tim should be arriving soon. I promised him I would make sure we got back pew seats, like good Presbyterians always do."

The lighter comment brought smiles and chuckles as he rose to head for the door. Ken walked him out. Sarah remained at the table, staring quietly out the window.

CHAPTER THIRTY

All took place with the centuries-old pageantry of the Church of England. At the end of the over an hour long service, the bishop, officials of the diocese, prominent priests, the Roman Catholic auxiliary bishop, and Father Frank processed back down the center aisle, followed by the casket and honored pallbearers, as the pipe organ continued strains of the last hymn, *For All the Saints*. Slowly, steadily, in stately formality, the casket was loaded into the back of the black Cadillac funeral hearse. Three matching black Cadillac limousines took in Sarah, Sally and her husband Ron, and Bill's surviving brother, then Ken and his family, and then the leading clergymen. The funeral procession left for the beautiful Allegheny Cemetery on Butler Street, with its rolling terrain and tall, old trees.

The historic cemetery was itself grand. It was the burial ground for 22 mayors of Pittsburgh, famous celebrities Stephen Foster, Lillian Russell, Josh Gibson and others. Many of the city's wealthy and prominent citizens were likewise interred there, as testified to by the elaborate statuary, tombstones, and mausoleums. Since it was on the National Registry of Historic Places, tours of the cemetery and the gravesites of famous people were conducted often. The Rev. Dr. William B. Brand would fit right in among them for his final resting place.

Danny drove alone in his Grand Cherokee in the long funeral procession. Tim had gone back to their church to wrap up preparations for the Sunday services since Danny would be up north in Michigan. At the cemetery, Danny followed Sarah's wishes and stood close behind the mourning family members, who were appropriately garbed in black. Sarah and Sally wore black, wide-brimmed hats and covered their faces with black veils. It was not Sarah's style to be so very formal, but she had yielded without protest to the rigorous tradition of high society.

The brief interment service was taken over by the bishop, but as the host pastor by default, Frank had an introductory part with invocation. At the conclusion, family members grabbed handfuls of the soil, tossed it onto the lowered casket in the vault, and the funeral director announced the conclusion of the graveside service. All present were invited back to Church of the Resurrection for the funeral luncheon, eulogy, and opportunity for condolences to be given to the family. At this point, some would not bother to return to the church. But since it was Dr. Brand, many would do so, especially church members, longtime friends, and by necessity, family.

As the graveside crowd of mourners began to disperse, Danny couldn't help but indulge his continuing sense of paranoia and glance over the cars lined up for a long way along the lane of the cemetery. He halfway expected to see a green Prius somewhere down the line, but shook his head at the thought. What would be the point to be there, if it did belong to the burglar or possible murderer? In any case, he didn't see one among all the Mercedes, a Rolls or two, at least one Bentley, numerous Cadillacs and other high end cars. He felt a little conspicuous with his Jeep, even though it was a Grand Cherokee.

The Fellowship Hall was mostly full, even though many had not returned to the church. The church ladies did themselves proud with a spread far beyond the usual funeral food of ham sandwiches and veggie plates. They and the caterer featured prime rib, salmon, chicken, a wide variety of side dishes, and more desserts than this crowd could possibly consume. Coffee hour after Sunday services this week would be blessed with lots of funeral leftovers, and much of it would also go over to the rectory for the Brand family.

Danny's eulogy was well-crafted, tasteful and laudatory, followed by tearful thanks from Sally and the other family members and "well done" from the few clergy who remained and many others. Bill had received about as fine a send-off into eternity as the Episcopal Church ever held, or anyone, for that matter.

Well into mid-afternoon, most of the mourners finished eating, expressed their sympathy, and left. The church ladies cleaned up the kitchen. The custodian, and a few church members with things to do around the church, remained to wrap things up. Then Sarah and her family members finally went over to the rectory to catch their breath. Danny was invited to join them, but he demurred.

"Ken and his family are going to be packing up to catch their flight this evening back to Houston," he said to Sarah. "Sally's finally going home to be with her husband. You'll be busy with them and need to collapse and get some rest before our road trip tomorrow. Why don't we touch base by phone later this evening?"

"That sounds good," Sarah said. "Give me a call maybe around nine-ish. Any later than that and I might be out like a light."

"Will do. I'm going home to pack some final things and rest myself."

A polite hug, a peck on the cheek in front of her family members, and Sarah saw Danny to the door of the church. They waved as he drove off.

CHAPTER THIRTY-ONE

They confirmed on the phone Friday night that he would pick her up at the rectory promptly at 7:00 Saturday morning. Like clockwork, Danny showed up at precisely 7:00. Sarah was still trying to get ready, so he took her two packed bags and loaded them into the back of the Jeep. As she applied finishing touches, he went around and checked windows and doors. All was locked. He noticed that the outside trash can by the garage was full, with a pastry box on top.

The church ladies had sent goodies and sheet cake pieces home with Sarah and her family. She tried to refuse politely, saying that they couldn't possibly use them, but the ladies had been really insistent, and obviously would have been offended if she didn't take the box. Danny thought briefly about trying to jam the box into the already-stuffed trash can so that no nosy woman from the church would see it sitting there and cluck about it, but Sarah was finally ready. It was going on 7:30 and they needed to hit the road.

They went north on I-79 to the Pennsylvania Turnpike, west until it turned into the Ohio Turnpike, all the way to the US 23 exit near Toledo. Weekend traffic was typically heavy, but there were a few less big trucks than during a typical work day. The weather continued to be good as it had been most of the week, and they crossed into Southeastern Michigan, exiting at the little town of Dundee to stop for a late fast food lunch. It would be another

265 miles or four and a half hours at least before they reached Traverse City in the northwest of the Lower Peninsula.

They traded off driving every couple of hours or so and used the time to reminisce and catch up on old times. Although such a long drive is tiring for anyone, all-in-all it was a refreshing break from the tension and extreme busyness of the past week. Sarah was her old self in most respects – although she napped different times during their travel. A sense of excitement, a genuine lift, filled the car as they crossed the border into Michigan. The most beautiful part of a beautiful state was still to the north of them, but there were more trees and more water to see as they continued to drive north.

Danny greatly enjoyed Sarah's renewed spirit as the miles went by, but he was frankly relieved that she didn't seem to press so closely to him. Their conversation was warm, like old friends, but he didn't sense the earlier feelings that she was wanting much more, including more intimacy from him. He had hoped that in her initial shock and grief she had merely been lapsing into very old feelings from their days as lovers. And it was also understandable that she felt scared and needy in her feeling of abandonment by Bill's death. But Danny had never wanted to take advantage in any way of some vulnerability on her part. They both needed time to process what had happened, and what was still happening.

Finally toward suppertime they approached Traverse City and its gorgeous bays. Danny had called ahead and made a reservation at Amical, one of the many excellent restaurants in town. They parked in the lot behind the building, on the other side of the famous Boardman River and walked over the river to the restaurant on a footbridge. They paused to look down on a trout fisherman spinning for spring steelhead in the current and looked out at the relaxing water of West Grand Traverse Bay with its multiple shades of blue.

Their table was ready and waiting for them since their arrival was just a few minutes earlier than their reservation time. They eased into the two chairs at the back window and both took deep breaths of relief. Danny ordered his favorite Canadian whiskey, Sarah a glass of local Boskydel red table wine from Leelanau County. He asked for the outstanding, locally-caught whitefish out of Lake Michigan; she went for the always well-prepared prime rib.

"I'm so glad you invited me to come with you to your cottage," Danny said. "I know it's been another exhausting day, but we're almost there, and while the time will be short, the trip itself is a great break for us."

"I agree," Sarah replied. "The cat naps in the car actually helped, and while the turnpikes and interstate highways didn't have a lot of appeal, once we headed north through Michigan I could feel healing taking place. The spring forest up this way is sensational. The trees all showing spring pastel colors of light green, red, yellow, blossoming and coming to life. And some trillium is showing up already on the forest floor. It's just lovely to see."

"Well, I'm sorry we couldn't be more leisurely in our travel. I bet if we had stopped by some of that trillium starting to open up with their white trumpets, we would have seen little woods violets and yellow trout lilies as well."

They took some time savoring their meal, enjoyed a cup of coffee after, and then Danny paid the bill. Back across the footbridge they got in his vehicle and set off on the last half-hour leg of their trip. From the edge of Traverse City they went north on M22, a northwestern Lower Peninsula state highway so popular and beautiful in its path that numerous cars they passed had diamond-shaped decals in black and white with simply "22" on back windows and tail gates.

Soon they reached the Grand Traverse County/Leelanau County line. Leelanau County is known as Michigan's "Little Finger," a large peninsula in its own right, extending up from the northwest corner of Michigan's "mitten-shaped" Lower Peninsula.

Not much more than 15 miles farther the Brand summer cottage sat on beautiful Stony Point, just outside the popular tourist town of Suttons Bay. Following Sarah's turn-by-turn directions, Danny soon pulled into the driveway of the Brands' cottage. It was set off Stony Point Road, down an asphalt drive that twisted a couple of times through thick trees, making the cottage scarcely visible from the road.

Once they stopped in front of it, Danny could see that "cottage" was an understatement. It was actually a large, four-bedroom, two-story summer home with considerable frontage on the shore of Grand Traverse Bay. North a good boat ride was the even more open water of Northern Lake Michigan. While not a brand-new construction, neither was the home very old. The Brands had engaged a leading architecture firm to design it so that it had a classic, old chateau appearance to it, but employed all the most modern and efficient features for energy conservation, state-of-the-art windows and doors, fireplaces that provided attractive fires but also efficient heating, tongue-and-groove hickory flooring throughout. The loveliness of the summer home was evident in every room.

He helped her with her bags, got her into the house, and lingered just a bit as she turned on lights and checked things out, turning on the thermostat as evening had brought temperatures edging into the high 30's. Danny paused before floor-to-ceiling windows in the great room overlooking Grand Traverse Bay. Miles across the bay lights twinkled and reflected off the rippling water. Pretty at night, it would be gorgeous tomorrow.

"Hey, I better get over to Leelanau Bed & Breakfast and check in there. If you're okay here," said Danny.

"I'm fine." Sarah replied. "I'm going to turn in so we can get as much done as possible tomorrow. I have Bill's things here to go through. At least he didn't keep his guns here. He feared a possible break-in and theft while we were in Pittsburgh. But he did keep boxes of shotgun shells and other shooting supplies so that he could shoot down at the Cedar Club. I'll want to get those things out of here, do some other things to make the place ready for possible listing. And I have some of my items that I want to take back to Pittsburgh on Monday."

"Sounds good, see you in the morning," Danny said. "Oh, I'll take a break late tomorrow morning and go over to the Cedar range. They have shotgun ranges open Sunday morning for shooting, and I want to talk to John Harrison about whether he observed Bill uncasing that 1100 trap gun with a choke tube already in place. I could take some of those shooting supplies over and either give them to interested members or have 'for sale' put up on the bulletin board."

"That would be helpful," Sarah replied, although with just a hint of a frown on her face. "Just give it to whoever can use the stuff; I don't care." She turned away abruptly.

Danny chalked up her attitude to a combination of tiredness and her distaste for anything associated with guns and shooting, which was even more understandable with what had happened to Bill. Another light hug and peck and he took off for the cozy bed and breakfast a few miles away. The breakfast part started serving at 6:00, so he'd get a sumptuous breakfast and be back at the Brand summer home by 7:00 to tackle the work that Sarah wanted done. He had wondered if she might try to coax him to stay at her place for the night, but was relieved that she didn't.

CHAPTER THIRTY-TWO

At 7:00 Sunday morning Danny rang the bell at Sarah's cottage. She came to let him in, obviously not long out of bed, greeted him in hastily donned sweats. The thought crossed his mind that she looked as alluring with baggy sweats and bunched up hair as she did in an evening dress and heels.

"Is it 7:00 already?" she protested. "Feels like the middle of the night."

"Sorry," he chuckled, "but we have a lot to do from the sounds of it. You point the way to Bill's shooting supplies, and I can start sorting and boxing and get it ready to take to the club when they open at 10:00. Then when you're ready, I'll help you with other things. I'm sure you're going to want your personal photos and artwork to take back to Pittsburgh, and we'll need to box those carefully. You keep summer clothes here, have kitchen items you want to take back..."

"Hold on, Speedy," she stopped him short. "Nothing happens until the coffee is brewed and some bagels are taken out of the freezer and toasted. I suppose you've already feasted this morning."

"Yeah, 'fraid so," Danny confessed. "But I put some fresh pastries in a bag to share with you. Here."

Sarah grabbed the bag. "Come on; pull up a stool at the kitchen island. You may not be completely forgiven for yanking me out of bed in the middle of the night, but this will help."

After coffee and sweet rolls, Danny got to work on Bill's shooting stuff – shooting vest, gloves, protective ear muffs, yellow-tinted glasses, and many other things that he had used over the years of shooting at the Cedar Rod & Gun Club. There were numerous boxes of shotshells, and a top-of-the-line Mec reloading machine for his 12 gauge 1100 shotgun. Occasionally Bill would shoot other gauges as well. He owned a sweet Fox 16 side-by-side, a matching 20 gauge Fox, a 28 gauge classic Ithaca, but he didn't bother reloading for those, simply buying cases of shells.

His money didn't make it necessary to reload at all. He could merely shoot factory loads all the time, but reloading was part of the fun of the sport, so, predictably, Danny found canisters of gunpowder, bags of lead shot, plastic wads, primers, all of the components to be able to reload empty shot shells. He got all those things ready and loaded in his vehicle.

The rest of the morning went quickly as he helped Sarah sort through things and pack up either to take back to Pittsburgh or to store and possibly sell later. A lot simply went into the trash. As they had while driving the day before, they talked pretty much non-stop, but Danny thought that she seemed a bit preoccupied, as though part of her mind was elsewhere. *She's probably remembering past fun here at their cottage and feeling a bit sad and wistful*, he thought. A couple of times she glanced out the window on the driveway side as she walked by.

"Expecting someone?" Danny asked.

"Oh, well," she paused, then went on. "I've been wondering if any of our neighbors here on the bay might be up. It's early in the season, and on both sides of us the folks don't usually open up their cottages until the beginning of May or so. But it's hard to tell, with all the woods shielding us from their places."

She stopped by the great room fireplace where Danny had started a fire with seasoned oak to help warm the place and stared at the flickering flames. Again it seemed obvious that she was briefly deep in thought and undoubtedly had fond memories.

It was almost 10:00, so Danny took his scheduled break, gave Sarah a little hug, and promised he'd be back before long. As he headed for the door he suggested take-out.

"I can pick up some of those huge burgers and fries you talk about from the Cedar Tavern on my way back and be here for lunch. Then we can go out for another relaxing supper this evening if you want."

"Super," she agreed. "I'll keep boxing things up 'til you get back."

"Oh," he said as he opened the door, "I forgot to say earlier that when I took off from the bed and breakfast this morning to head over here, I was in a hurry and absentmindedly left my cell phone on the dresser in my room. So if you would have any reason to call me, call the number of the range house at the gun club. I should be there in 30 minutes or so."

"Will do," Sarah called after him. "But, I'll be fine."

She walked back to that driveway window and watched as he backed around and took off. After she turned away from the window and back toward the torn-apart kitchen, a green Prius drove by slowly on Stony Point Road.

CHAPTER THIRTY-THREE

Danny arrived at the Cedar Rod & Gun Club about 10:15. Squads of shooters were already on the skeet and 5-stand ranges, firing away in turn. He entered the range house, where George the range master looked at him inquiringly.

"Welcome to the Cedar Rod & Gun Club. You looking for someone?"

"Thank you," Danny replied. "I'm Daniel Henriks. I've never been here before, but my friend Dr. Brand shot here when up at his cottage."

"That's right; he's a member. Are you meeting him here today?"

"I really wish we were." Danny proceeded to fill George in on the fact of Bill's death just a week ago, without going into the details of just how he had died.

He added, "This is a box is full of shooting supplies – protective ear muffs, a fine Beretta shooting vest, some boxes of shotgun shells, and a number of other items – which Bill's widow wanted to donate to the club, for anyone who might like to use them."

George accepted the box with thanks.

"But, I can't tell you how sorry I am to hear about his death. Wow, what a shocker. Dr. Brand was always a real gentleman. And a good shot. Loved his old Remington 1100 trap gun."

"Actually," Danny said, "I'm here in part to inquire about that gun. I understand he was here on an early spring vacation just last month and shot a few rounds. Did you notice if he shot with that gun?"

"This is a gun club," George laughed. "We always notice who's shooting with what. And if a member shows up with a new gun, guys will cluster around him to get a look at it faster than a bunch of grandmothers around a young lady with a new baby. Well, maybe not quite that fast." George chuckled again at his joke. "Sure, he shot with the 1100, and a round of skeet with his 20 gauge side-by-side. Really liked the old, classic shotguns."

"Now this might seem like a funny question," Danny went on. "But did you also notice if he uncased it with a choke tube already in place, or did he screw in the choke tube after he uncased it, just before going out to shoot?"

"Dr. Brand always did things the same way, like a ritual. He would uncase the 1100, open the action so that anyone could see that it was unloaded, carefully lay it on the open case, reach in his shooting gear bag, take out a plastic case with his choke tubes, select one, then screw it in, then set the gun in the gun rack just outside the door of the range house here...until he and his squad of shooters were ready to walk down to the range and begin shooting. Never, ever, changed the order of his preparations before shooting."

"You're sure?"

"Sure as the sun rises. Well, sure as shooting," George laughed at himself again.

Danny furrowed his brow and mulled George's words over for a moment. The itch in his mind flared up again. No way did it make sense that Bill would have stopped to take out a choke tube from its case and screw it in if he really wanted to stick the muzzle in his mouth and kill himself. Unless he did it robotically, just out of irresistible habit. No, Bill's selection of which choke tube to use was always related to what it was he was about to shoot. Open choke for closer range, medium choke for medium range, tighter choke for longer range....very intentional. There would have been no range consideration with committing suicide by the manner in which he had died. Nope. No reason. No way, he would have done that.

"George," Danny went on, "I'm supposed to meet that gun fitter, John Harrison, here this morning. Have you seen him yet?"

"Sure thing. He's out on 5-stand, in the first squad of the morning. It goes fast, so they'll be done and back in the house here pretty quick while the next squad goes out. You're more than welcome to hang out; talk to the guys waiting; admire someone's new gun." George chuckled again.

In a few minutes the 5-stand shooters walked into the range house, adding to the noise of multiple conversations with loud comments about who hit what great shot on a tough double, and who blew an easy, straightaway target. Danny looked over to George nearby.

"That's him, the tall guy with a bit of a beard," George said.

Danny walked over to introduce himself to the legendary gun fitter and stock bender.

"I'm Danny Henriks," he said, shaking John's offered hand. "Thanks for agreeing to meet me." He had called Harrison Friday evening before their trip, after finding his number in Bill's Rolodex.

"What can I do for you?" John asked. "You're here all the way from Pennsylvania?"

"I am. I'm a long-time friend and colleague of Bill Brand and a fellow shooter. Before I ask my questions, you probably haven't heard about Bill's death."

"Golly, no. What happened?"

Danny proceeded to tell him about Bill being found on the floor of his study at his church with his 1100 shotgun on the rug next to him.

"The police are saying it was by his own hand," Danny added.

"Well, I guess you never know what's going on in another fella's head, but that doesn't sound like the Dr. Brand I knew and shot with here at Cedar. When he was up here about a month ago I even did some quick adjustment to that gun for him. Added a new recoil pad, just a bit thicker, to ease the recoil and lengthen the trigger pull for him slightly. Made a better fit, and he immediately felt it shot a bit better. Of course," John added, "changing a gun fit ever so slightly for a shooter will usually make him feel more optimistic, even if it's not really significant." He smiled knowingly.

"I'd like to ask you the same questions I asked George over behind the counter," said Danny. He repeated his query about Bill's handling of his shotgun prior to shooting a round of trap, and whether he had changed his practice of putting in a choke tube as a last preparation before walking out to the range.

"Actually," John replied, "Dr. Brand and I discussed that and other things related to his shooting preparation more than once, including last month. I advised him to keep a strict routine. Clay target shooting is such a head game; you want everything to be as automatic as possible. Your focus should be entirely on the target as it's coming out of the trap; don't even think about should I be doing this or that differently before shooting. With these modern guns, semi-auto snap caps aren't even necessary, but since he was used to using them with older guns, it was just part of his routine. And as far as the choke tubes are concerned, there would be no reason to have one screwed in while carrying the gun in its case. For one thing, when he was about to go out to the trap range to shoot, he might very well decide to put in a different tube than what he had in mind, depending on wind or other variables."

"So," Danny summed it up, "he always did the same thing and carried his gun without a choke tube while in its case."

"Absolutely. While it may seem like a small matter, like I said, keep your routine set and just concentrate on the shooting itself. The less to think about, the better."

"I really appreciate your giving me your time," Danny thanked him and shook his hand again.

"Any time," John said. "And I sure am sorry to hear about him dying. He was a good man. But you're welcome to come here and shoot as a guest whenever you can."

"I appreciate the invitation. Not this trip, I'm afraid, but maybe next time." Danny left with a friendly wave to George and walked back to his Grand Cherokee feeling certain and determined. There was no way that Bill's death was a suicide

CHAPTER THIRTY-FOUR

Danny stopped as planned at the Cedar Tavern and got cheeseburgers, fries, and ginger ale to go for Sarah and him. As he waited for his order, received it, and paid, his mind churned about his total conviction that Bill Brand had been murdered in his church. He jumped back into his car and drove faster than usual back to Stony Point.

The half-hour drive back to the Brand summer home would have been a delight for Danny under other circumstances. The Leelanau Peninsula is home to lots of beautiful wildlife occupying its woods, water, farms, vineyards and orchards, and a big whitetail doe stood in the roadside ditch, munching on fresh, spring grass as he drove by on the county road. A flock of wild turkeys crossed in front of him. He passed by a bald eagle nest as he approached West Grand Traverse Bay. The white-headed mature male and female had probably recently returned north to produce two young fledglings, like their counterparts near Pittsburgh .

But, he barely noticed all that natural wonder as he turned over and over in his mind his renewed conviction that Bill could not have committed suicide. It hadn't made sense before, and now it made even less sense. He was determined to convince Sarah of that conclusion, and thought hard about how to get a more thorough investigation underway on the part of the police in Pittsburgh.

He pulled into the drive and parked in the same place in front of the two-car garage attached to the house, first turning around so that the tailgate was close to the garage door. It would make it easier to load boxes, household items, and some of her luggage for the return trip tomorrow morning. Sarah had taken his advice and locked the front door, although it seemed odd, since lots of people in that very low-crime area didn't bother locking doors. He used the key she had given him, walked in the entryway, and called for her.

"I'm upstairs boxing up the summer clothes we kept here. Almost done. I'll be right down," she hollered.

Still holding their lunch take-out bags, Danny walked over to the great room and looked out at the bay. Then he turned to a side window. Trying to peer through the screening trees, he caught just a glimpse of what seemed to be a car in the back driveway of the neighbors to the north. It hadn't been there before. It looked like...a lime-green subcompact.

Keeping his intent stare on the distant car as the tree branches swayed in the wind and obscured his line of sight, Danny hollered up to Sarah, "Sarah, come down here. Did you see a little green car up at the neighbor's...?"

A sharp blow to the back of his head caught Danny completely by surprise. He hadn't heard the faint footsteps coming up behind him. Stunned but still conscious, he whirled clumsily to try to engage his attacker. He swung at a man dressed in black, striking his hooded cheek, trying desperately to fend off another blow aimed at his head again. The assailant missed with his second try, enabling Danny to push the man around and grab him from behind. But his attacker rolled quickly, breaking Danny's grip, and landed a kick to Danny's chest that sent him crashing into the lamp table near the window. Teetering on the brink of unconsciousness, he tried to rise and strike back, but for the second time in a week, Danny's world turned black from another blow from the wooden club the man wielded.

CHAPTER THIRTY-FIVE

Danny had no idea how much time had passed before he started to regain consciousness. First he heard a man's voice, although he had trouble making out the words. Then his blurred vision started to discern rough shapes and some movement. He shook his head, trying to clear cobwebs from his brain and blinked several times to try to regain focus in his vision. He couldn't help but moan faintly with the pain. It cannot be good to suffer two concussions in less than a week's time.

At his pained groan the man walked over toward him from the other side of the great room. "Ah, he seems to be coming out of it. He has a hard head, the Rev. Dr. Henriks."

Danny feebly tried to form words. "Who...what..." and then his fearful concern emerged as it had at Tiny's office last Tuesday. "Sarah," he called weakly, "Sarah, are you...?"

His assailant interrupted. "Sarah's fine. You needn't worry about her."

A hint of recognition fought its way into Danny's struggling consciousness. The voice, the voice seemed familiar. He blinked hard again, trying to see who it was that was speaking to him. At the same time, he tried to move his arms and legs, but couldn't. He was restrained by duct tape, binding his arms and wrists behind him and tying him to one of the dining table chairs in the center of the great room. More duct tape bound his ankles to the legs of the chair. To restrain him further, a rope had been tied around his chest and around the straight back of the chair.

"Where is she?" Danny finally managed the words. "What have you done with her? If you've hurt her..." However feebly, he tried to move and rise up toward his captor, but couldn't.

"Now there's no use getting yourself all lathered up. You can't go anywhere. Besides, I told you she's fine. You, however, are not."

And the man leaned forward, close to Danny's bruised face, dripping with small cuts from the broken lamp and vase that had been on the table. He grabbed Danny's chin with a forceful grip and tilted his head up. Blinking again, Danny was finally able to see something...and gazed weakly into the face of Father Frank Lewis.

CHAPTER THIRTY-SIX

Father Frank pushed Danny's head down again roughly and spun around and walked toward the curving staircase going up to the second-floor bedrooms and baths. "He's awake now," he called up to someone. Then he strode back in Danny's direction. Now Danny could see that he was wearing his Episcopal priest's plain, black suit, with black shoes...and a black clerical shirt with a small white tab at the throat of the plain band of a collar. Young Frank had followed his rector's lead in dressing very traditionally and conservatively. But while Bill had done so for professional purposes, preferring flannel and stonewashed canvas shirts and blue jeans in his off time, Frank was more of a purist, dressing in his black priest's garb almost all the time, even away from church duties. He wanted everyone to know that he was a priest of the Church and that he should be addressed as "Father."

Semi-coherent thoughts tried to form in Danny's battered brain. It had to have been Frank ransacking Bill's home study last Tuesday night. But why? Why would he want to steal his boss's precious papyrus fragment? And if it was Frank who had been shadowing him, or them, in a green Prius...well, Frank drove an old Volvo four-door sedan. And how did Frank end up here in Northern Michigan? Had he followed the two of them all the way from Pittsburgh? And then the most horrible thought squeezed its way into Danny's confused thinking. Was it Frank, then, who had killed Bill Brand? But why? Bill had been a fatherly mentor to young Frank.

Danny's worry about what Frank might have done to Sarah finally shut off the flood of other thoughts and questions. With Frank leaning on the edge of the table in front of him, Danny tried again.

"Where's Sarah?" Then more strongly than he felt capable of, "You better not have hurt her. What have you done with her?"

"He hasn't done anything with me, Daniel." Sarah had come down the stairs and walked toward them. "Actually, he's done *for* me." She reached Frank's side, took his arm, looked up at him sweetly, and gave him a loving kiss on his cheek...while Frank kept his menacing glare directed at a captive who was clearly no threat to anyone. It seemed that Frank was still angry at the wild punch Danny had landed to the side of his face, making a red mark.

"You should go up and put on some casual clothes, sweetheart. Your priest's garb makes you stand out too much up here in the North Woods. I laid out a comfy sweater and jeans for you. Go on, I'll keep our busybody under guard. He's not going anywhere. At least not yet." She smiled ominously.

Frank wheeled and left them, and Sarah turned her attention back to Danny.

"Daniel, Daniel, why did you have to be so compulsively stubborn. Why couldn't you accept what everyone else did, that my pig of a husband killed himself out of shame? Now look at you."

His fog lifting, Danny looked up at her with glazed vision. "Frank Lewis killed Bill?"

"No, silly, I killed Bill."

"Why, Sarah? You seemed so happy, the two of you."

"That's what everyone seemed to think. And yes, Bill's family money gave me a lot of fun and satisfaction over the years, but he certainly didn't. He gave his time and attention to everything and everyone else in his life. He spent sixty, seventy hours a week with his church involvements. He had to serve on every community board and high-profile committee – from Rotary to the board of directors of Red Cross. He spent all kinds of time on his archeology projects – from the Kelso museum to going on digs in the Holy Land. He even spent time with you at the shooting range. He was always unavailable."

"But to shoot him in his church?"

Sarah vented on, almost as if she didn't hear his question, "Oh, we could have maintained the pretense of our marriage and continued to live our separate lives under the same roof. In our early years I thought having a child or two would at least give me that satisfaction, but he was sterile, so that wasn't going to happen. But then there was the ridiculous cliché of his affair with the organist. He didn't have time for me, but he could bang her in his study at the church. I could deal with the estrangement, but that betrayal with that twit on the organ bench was the last straw. The three of us kept it quiet from everyone else, but I walked in on them one day, and I could never forgive him for it."

"But why not just get a divorce?" Danny asked.

"Oh, no. I wasn't going to settle for half of his assets. After all those years and that final humiliation, I wanted every dollar of the family money that he had parked in the Caymans. And I certainly wasn't going to be the poor divorcee that everyone pitied. No, he would seem to commit suicide, and I would be the rich widow. But you couldn't leave it alone, Daniel. Everyone else could, but no, not you."

Frank came back down in his sweater and blue jeans. He ignored Danny trussed up in his chair and spoke to Sarah. "Do you want me to gas up the Bayliner so that it's ready to go tonight?'

"Yes," she agreed. "But make sure that no one's around and watching you. Keep the boat in the boathouse with the doors closed, so that no one going by on the bay can see you working on it. Check all the instruments, running lights, and by all means, the plug. We don't want to have to be bailing water out there tonight. Wait until after dark before moving our luggage and supplies down to the garage. The neighbors on either side aren't up here this early in the spring, but there's no sense taking any chances on a surprise visit from them."

"You got it, love," Frank said, and he slipped out the lakeside door after looking carefully for anyone nearby. He quickly stepped into the boat house and smiled at the big Bayliner Cruiser, equipped with a diesel engine, comfortable sleeping quarters, a galley, private head, and all the features for long-distance, multiple-day cruises on the big lake – all for just over $75,000.

"I have some things to do, Daniel, before we're all ready for tonight's trip. Be a good boy and just let your poor head clear quietly. Frank will be a while down at the boathouse, but I'll be back in a few." And at that she reached for the roll of duct tape, pulled off a strip, and slapped it over his mouth. "There. Nobody's close enough to hear you even if you scream your pounding head off, but if you would want to try, I don't want to hear it." She headed back upstairs.

Despite wanting to stay alert and think of some way to get loose, Danny could feel himself slipping back toward unconsciousness. His head slumped down and everything turned black again.

CHAPTER THIRTY-SEVEN

After finishing her packing and other preparations, Sarah left the things in the upstairs hall and went down and out to the boathouse to check on Frank. He was busily occupied and said that he would be back up to the cottage in about an hour or so. She returned to the great room and their bound captive.

Danny was stirring and groaning again, so she removed the duct tape from his mouth, slapped him sharply on his cheek, and roused him back to semi-consciousness. "I'll leave the tape off your mouth for a bit so long as you don't get rowdy. Want some water?"

He nodded weakly. In a matter of seconds she was back from the kitchen with a glass of water. She tilted his head back a bit and poured a bit of the cold water down his throat.

"Feeling a twinge of compassion?" Danny asked, clearing his throat and licking his sore lips.

"Not at all. Just figured you might want to ask me how this all happened, and I'm pleased to tell you."

"Okay," Danny proceeded, thinking to the best of his ability how he could keep her talking, maybe awaken some compassion, some memories, some of the love that Sarah had once professed for him, something within her to want to keep him alive and not make him another murder. "How...how did you stage it to look like a suicide?"

"Bill had gone over to his Rector's Study Saturday night to review his Easter sermon and other parts of the liturgy. I told him that I would go over after the 9:00 television program I wanted to watch, that I had a surprise for him. By a little after 10:00 I went over there, no one else was in the church that late, with a full bottle of his favorite 18-year-old single malt scotch and a couple of crystal tumblers.

"He had been so giddy and preoccupied with his stupid papyrus find that I told him he should take a moment to have a bit of celebration. I had taken the thing out of his hidden compartment of his desk at home, and brought the leather packet to his church study and put it on his desk in front of him. He started to be extremely upset that I had taken it out, but I told him that I wanted to see it. So I asked him to undo the packet, and we'd both lift a glass to his great accomplishment. I knew he wanted to, but he hesitated because the next morning was Easter Sunday, and he wanted to be at his best for his precious congregation. Besides, he still considered himself a recovering alcoholic, keeping his drinking under control. At least maybe we should have a celebratory glass back in the rectory, he suggested, instead of in his church study.

"I said not to be silly. No one was around, and besides, I wanted to see it with him, because I was so proud of him. At that he agreed, and I poured a good half-glass of the scotch for each of us. He raised his eyebrows at my generous pour, but feeling more in the spirit of the occasion, took it and sipped it vigorously.

"Well, you know how in the old days Bill liked to talk and drink and talk and drink, so I kept asking him to tell me again just how he found it in the first place, how he knew it was so important, how it had been rigorously tested...everything I could think of that I knew he would love to go on and on about regarding the ragged piece of crap. So he kept expounding, and I kept pouring, and forgetting just how much he was chugging down, he kept talking and drinking. With too much to drink, he always became even more boringly verbose, so I hardly listened, but I kept smiling, nodding, encouraging him to go on. I kept pouring.

"At one point it dawned on him in his increasingly fuzzy state that he was drinking too much, and tried to say that we had better go back to the rectory, but I had saved a vital question for just that tipping point. I insisted that he tell me about the repercussions that would sound through Christendom as a result of his making the fragment of shit public. He tried to rally at that call to battle, but as he pontificated on changing the course of Christian history, he just couldn't make whole sentences anymore, and finally his head slumped down on his folded arms on his desk. He started snoring like the sorry drunk he was."

Danny couldn't believe what was coming out of Sarah's mouth. Even in his blurry state, he was appalled beyond description. But he had to keep her talking. "And then you went and got the shotgun?"

"Of course. I had gotten it out of his gun safe down in our basement. He insisted that I know the combination and how to access a handgun for my protection when he was gone on his many trips. That was when I made my mistake that you stumbled on with your irritating nosiness. I had only seen the shotgun at the cottage here when he insisted that I go along with him to that Cedar place. And when I saw it there, it had that choke thing on the end of the barrel, so when I took it out of the safe, I thought I had to screw in one of his several chokes in order to use it properly. I tucked it in our kitchen pantry until I needed it."

"I brought it over to the church in complete darkness, no outside lights for anyone to be able to see me go back and forth. I had been completely careful not to touch anything in the study except the scotch bottle and glasses, and when I returned I had gloves on and wiped the bottle clean of my prints and then placed his limp hand on it to leave only his. His glass I left as he had left it; mine I removed, of course. I took off his shoe and sock, stuck his big toe against the trigger, removed it, placed his hands around the stock and barrel, removed them, lifted his head back against the back of his desk chair, stuck the barrel of the shotgun in his gaping mouth...and pressed the trigger. I have to admit that I was startled at the gunshot and the blood and tissue that exploded, and I dropped the gun to the floor as his body tumbled out of the chair and onto that Persian rug he was so proud of, but I was going to toss the gun down there, anyway."

As much as her descriptive details and his aching head combined to nauseate Danny, he was determined to keep her talking. Even though describing her murderous act seemed to stir up her anger and resentment more than any hint of softness and compassion.

"But there was a horrible spray of blood and gore. Didn't you get any of that on you?" Danny wondered.

"I had thought of that," Sarah seemed actually to brag. "I covered myself with a foldable plastic rain parka and made especially sure not to step in the spray and pool of blood. Almost all of the blood went back from his head, of course, but I looked around to see if any droplets had blown back in my direction. There were very few, so on close examination I could tell that my outline would not be left in an absence of blood spray in front of him. There was absolutely no evidence that I, or anyone else for that matter, had been there that night. If the police did find any of my prints elsewhere in the study, well, there would be who knows how many others as well. A lot of people went in and out to see him there, staff members and others every day."

"And you just left him there. How heartless." Danny knew that Sarah might push back at his accusation of her callousness, but whatever direction her thoughts and feelings were going, he wanted her to keep talking. And she seemed perfectly glad to do so.

"Heartless! He was the one who was heartless. He broke *my* heart. He and that damn demanding congregation. Sure, it would have been easier to do it in his study at home, but I wanted them to suffer, too. I wanted them to know that their taking and taking and taking from him – and cruelly, from me – had driven Bill to take his own life. And committing suicide in their church would make a statement. A statement they would never forget. An Easter they would never forget."

Danny shook his head painfully for more than one reason. "But Sarah..."

"I think that's enough questions for now," she erupted angrily and slapped the tape back over his mouth. She left the great room again and went down to the boathouse, leaving him trying to look around for a way out of a situation that felt ever more hazardous to his life.

CHAPTER THIRTY-EIGHT

With both Frank and Sarah down at the boathouse, Danny was desperate to find a way free himself. There was nothing on the big dining room table that might cut through the duct tape. Maybe he could find a letter opener or scissors at the entryway table. But the kitchen seemed like the best bet. He wiggled his chair back and forth, clumsily but gradually working it across the hickory wood floor toward the kitchen. It seemed to take forever. He kept glancing toward the side door that led out and down toward the boathouse. Finally, he reached the kitchen counter.

He remembered the drawer under the counter that held knives and kitchen scissors, and by straining he was able to rise a bit with his bound feet and force his duct-taped hands back and up to reach for the drawer pull. He didn't quite reach it, and with his head pounding and his heart racing, he thumped the chair down on the imported ceramic tile floor. He tried again, then again. He was just about able to grasp it.

The door out to the boathouse opened, and Sarah came back in the house. An expression of surprise appeared on her face as she quickly spotted Danny trussed up in his chair near the kitchen drawer.

She laughed as she said, "Oh, no, Daniel. That's being a naughty boy. I don't think you'd have been able to cut your way out even if I had handed you a knife to use, but I suppose you had to try. We need you to stay where you were."

She wrestled the chair and Danny back toward the dining table at the center of the great room, bumping and scraping on the floor the whole way.

Danny was thoroughly exhausted with his effort and the effect of his latest concussion. He snorted through his nostrils, trying to get his breath. Sarah ripped the tape off his mouth, clearly angry at his trying to find a way to escape.

"There," she said, "you want to breathe more easily? Fine. We want to keep you functioning at least a while longer. Frank's just about done with the boat. Then we wait until well after dark for your trip."

Gasping and gulping in air, Danny couldn't think of anything but to try to get Sarah talking again. Some change of mind and heart needed to click in with her, or he feared more and more that he would be joining Bill in Eternity.

"What about Frank? How does he figure into all this?"

"Oh, Frank," she laughed cynically. "When I walked in on Bill and organist twit in his study almost two years ago – yes, it was after he had returned from Jerusalem with that waste of a fortune in his hands – I decided that two could play that game."

"So you seduced Frank?" asked Danny, starting to regain his breath.

"It was surprisingly easy. The young man was wound pretty tight, but he loosened up bit by bit, started to enjoy my attention, and I think became enamored with the idea of this rich cougar finding him irresistible. He rather chafed being under Bill's thumb, anyway, and I played on that, telling him that he had far too much talent to have to take Bill's criticisms and overbearing direction as his boss. I also shared more and more how miserable Bill made me, how actually abusive Bill was, and how I wished I had someone to rescue me."

"And he fell for that?"

"Fell for it? He lapped it up like the little doggy he is. Although, I have to admit, I had almost forgotten how energetic a young man can be in bed. I couldn't bed him in the rectory, of course, but then, that's what cheap motels are for. It's gone on for just about a year now, so he's absolutely convinced that I love him and want him to take me away from all my misery."

"So it was Frank in his priest's garb going through Bill's study at home last Tuesday night when you and I interrupted him."

"Yes," Sarah confirmed. "I had gone back to the rectory Saturday night after I shot Bill, of course, and I took the papyrus with me, but I needed to have someone else to blame for the disappearance of the wretched scrap, so I convinced Frank to stage a break-in and ransacking of the home study. It would appear as though the papyrus was taken that night."

"But what did you do with the papyrus?"

Sarah waved her hand dismissively. "I burned it in the fireplace that Saturday night. What good was it, anyway? Just more stirring of the religious pot, getting people fussed up for nothing. It was just one more thing that took Bill away from me and wasted a lot of money that could have been well-spent somewhere else."

Despite Danny's dangerous predicament, he felt a painful sense of loss at hearing about Sarah's destruction of the unique archeological treasure. To think that such a significant find would be so callously destroyed. It had survived almost two thousand years, but now was nothing but ash. He sighed and slumped, but then snapped his head up as fear of his plight took over again.

"What do the two of you plan to do with me?"

"Ah, Daniel," it was her turn to sigh. "This can't end well for you. You make me practically as angry and frustrated as I was with Bill all those years. He's finally out of the way, and I let you know how our old romance still smoldered inside of me, but you have to be so proper and righteous. You couldn't show a spark of interest. This could have been you and I getting ready to motor off to a new and luxurious life with Bill's stashed-away millions. And maybe I could have rekindled something within you in time, but you had to keep poking at the manner of Bill's death. Nobody else cared about that stupid choke thing in the shotgun. So now you're a liability that has to be eliminated."

"No, Sarah, think about what you're saying. You don't really want to kill me. We've been friends all these years. Remember way back in our Pitt days, don't they mean anything to you anymore? And all those times the three of us were together over the years, you have to have some fondness for the good times."

Sarah seemed totally unmoved by his pleas, and continued to rattle on.

"Frank, too, actually. He's been a good lap dog, but his purpose has been served. He tailed you to see just what trouble you were up to. He was going to do it in his old Volvo, but I pointed out that you could well recognize his car, so he borrowed his younger brother's green Prius for the week. The kid lives in Mt. Washington and uses public transportation to and from the Pitt campus. Parking's such a bitch, you know. We had no way of knowing that that Father John also drives a green Prius, and that you'd fixate on it. Frank did have the idea of stealing someone else's plates, so that if you took down the license number, it wouldn't trace back to his brother, and eventually himself."

"Frank is so gullible, I'm afraid." Sarah continued. "He thinks that he and I are going to deal with you, then go back to Pittsburgh, make necessary preparations and arrangements, and flee to Samoa, live happily on a tropical island for the rest of our lives on Bill's money. He's right about the Samoa part. For me, not for him, sad to say."

Danny reacted to her continued callousness by desperately thinking of something to do. If he couldn't get free himself, maybe he could at least let Frank know that they were both in danger.

Samoa does not have an extradition treaty with the United States. With electronic access to Bill's family money in a secure and confidential account in the Caymans, Sarah could grease whatever Samoan officials' palms might be necessary to keep herself shielded from even the possibility of prosecution. Eventually the police would start to figure out what happened to Frank and to him, and eventually to Bill, and she would go from black widow to serial killer.

Again, Sarah seemed actually to take pleasure in sharing the details of her brutal murder, and her plans for two more, so she continued.

"Poor little Frank will help me get you down to the boat later tonight, when all is dark and our activity invisible. He thinks that we're going to dump you out in the bay with a bullet in your head, then come back here and take off for Pittsburgh for our next steps to the grand, new life together in the South Pacific. He has the first part right. What he doesn't know is that he won't get back to the cottage."

"I told him to be sure to check the drain plug in the boat. Since he has surely done so, he won't bother to look at it again. I will take it out before we even motor out with you. Once a few miles out in the big water, we'll deposit you with the fish, I will cut the fuel line for the boat without him seeing it. As he tries and tries again to start the motor, I will slip on my wetsuit and make a pretense of getting into the water to check the prop and mechanisms down there. Meanwhile, the stalled boat will constantly be taking on water and start floundering. By the time he notices that he's sinking, I'll be swimming back to shore. Frank can't swim very well, so he'll surely drown out there. He'll call for help, call for me, I'm sure, but that late, out on that distant black water, no one will hear. Maybe the two of you will be together forever."

"And you don't think the police will link you to his death and mine?" Danny asked, still incredulous about all that he was hearing.

"No, I've thought of that, too. Once back here in the cottage, I'll dry off, wait a bit, then use this duct tape on my own wrists and ankles. I'll rub them until they look red and raw, cut through but leave tape in place, and then give myself a real bonk on my head with that wooden club Frank used on you. I'll call the sheriff and report that a burglar broke in, subdued and taped both of us, then took off in the boat with you, I don't know to where or why. I eventually worked myself free and called them in tears and hysteria."

"And when they investigate, they'll eventually find the sunken boat, Frank's body and mine." Danny concluded for her. "And since he drowned, it will look like he murdered me, but didn't realize the drain plug was missing and went down with the ship. Looks like you've thought of everything, except..." He still hoped he could keep her talking and himself alive.

"Except what?"

"What about the cut fuel line to the motor?" That will show foul play. It won't work, Sarah. In the end result they'll piece it together and figure out that it was your doing. You should rethink this and let me go, please"

"Nice try, preacher boy. That fuel line is old and showing cracks in the surface. When I cut it, it'll be by scraping, and it will look like age and friction just wore a hole. Oh, I suppose if their techs analyze it carefully enough they can see through it, but I'll sell our mutual captivity well enough that they may not even look that closely. Especially since evidence on me will show rape on the part of that lustful young Episcopal priest. He was doing away with the both of us to try to hide his crimes. In any case, by the time anyone would bother to look deep enough, the mourning widow will be enjoying her new life in extradition-free Samoa."

"The two of you had sex here just now?"

"Danny, what do you suppose lover-boy and I were doing while you were at the gun club? Thanks for bringing back lunch, by the way. Too bad it ended up scattered across the floor when our attacker fought with you. Well enough of this." She re-taped Danny's mouth.

CHAPTER THIRTY-NINE

Frank came through the door from the boathouse. "Everything's ready. Shall we wrestle him down there?"

"No, not yet," Sarah replied. "I have our bags ready upstairs for our trip tomorrow morning, but we should wait until, oh, about 11:00 before taking him out there. By that time anyone who might be home down the shore a way should be either in bed or watching the late news. We don't want to take the slightest chance of anyone seeing the boat go out. And if we leave the boathouse and the shallows with no-wake, slow speed, no one will hear anything, either."

Danny wiggled around in his chair and looked pleadingly at Frank, shaking his head in an obvious "no-no" motion.

"Settle down, Danny-boy," Frank snarled at him. "You've made enough trouble for us already. We don't need your pathetic struggles and clamor. You should save what strength you still have for praying to the God you will soon be going to."

What Danny was praying for just then was for someone to come to the summer home for some reason and that he could raise enough fuss to get their attention. Or failing that, at least that Sarah and Frank would go up to the master bedroom for another session – more fake-rape for Sarah – and be so occupied with each other's pleasures that they would leave him alone for another try at the kitchen drawer.

He continued to look up at Frank as pleadingly as he could, but Frank seemed oblivious to Danny's strained look to him. And even though Frank had said very little to him since their fight, the young priest finally seemed motivated to say something to Danny about his part in this captivity and planned murder.

"I'm sure that the great Rev. Dr. Henriks is wondering why this is happening to him. Well, you were so buddy-buddy with Bill Brand, and I got sick and fed up with him coaching me and saying, 'You should take notes when Dr. Henriks is preaching, how his illustrations capture the inner meaning of the Scripture. You should stand nearby when Dr. Henriks is greeting people at meetings, notice how he always addresses them by name and inquires about their spouse or family or work or some other personal matter. You should make an appointment with Dr. Henriks and ask him how he approaches directing his staff.' Well, if he thought you had all the answers, he should have taken you on to be his co-pastor instead of hiring me as his flunky assistant. And if that wasn't bad enough, I had that fussy old Margaret ordering me around, a mere secretary acting like she was the priest and I was her errand boy."

Frank paused for a breath, then continued. "And then, when Sarah recognized my talent and abilities and we fell in love, and she finally gives the old bastard what he deserved for the way he treated her, you come along and meddle and can't give it a rest about how he died. And you tried to turn her head with your charm. Whether it was my professional life or my personal life, you had to be in the way. Well, tonight you're in the way for the last time, Danny-boy."

And with a hostility that Danny never suspected, Frank gave him another blow to the side of his head, and he could feel the pain and blackness coming back. Frank and Sarah did leave the great room as Danny had been hoping, but in his unconsciousness he couldn't even attempt an effort to free himself.

CHAPTER FORTY

A few hours passed before Danny started to come out of the blackness. Although he had no way of knowing the time, the early spring sun had set and left the tall windows of the great room looking out on a darkening twilight. Very faint, flickering lights appeared sparsely on the opposite shore of the big bay, but Danny had trouble seeing much of anything with his blurry vision.

For hours now, practically the whole afternoon and now obviously into the evening, he had been cruelly bound to this chair. His muscles in his arms and legs were cramping. The fragmented thought struggled through his mind that even if he could somehow free himself, he might very well collapse just trying to get up. He doubted he possessed the ability to stand up, much less run away.

As his thinking started to function again, however laboriously, he desperately speculated about how anyone might find him in the next few hours. Mildred and Tim Murphy knew that he had gone on this trip with Sarah, but they weren't expecting him back at South Presbyterian until the morning after tomorrow. The earliest they would expect even to hear from him on a status update would be sometime tomorrow, and in the unlikely event that they would be concerned about him not calling, that would be too late. In the busyness of his professional life over the years, this was the first time he had felt so alone in his personal life. There was literally no one to worry about where he was, or what might be happening to him.

He had to fight this concussion-related depression and loneliness. Although a way to escape, or to convince his bitter captors to release him, eluded his scrambled thinking, Danny Henriks refused to surrender. Hope and faith was what made life worth living, and he just couldn't give up on life, much less on the God in whom he believed.

Whatever Sarah and Frank had been doing, maybe it really was more sex, they returned just then to the kitchen, which was open to the great room, separated only by a large, granite kitchen island with wooden stools. They heated cups of coffee, put some frozen pizza in the oven, then perched on two of the stools and looked out at poor Danny.

"Should we remove the tape from his mouth so that he can plead for his life. Or say his fond farewells?" Frank snickered.

That was definitely a potential complication that Sarah didn't want. In the unlikely event that Danny could find the words to put a miniscule of doubt in Frank's mind, she didn't want to have to deal with it.

"No," she answered, "he's been far too much of a distraction all along. Leave him be. Although he does make a rather dramatic decoration for the great room," she mocked. They both laughed at his plight.

"Should we leave his Jeep in the garage?" Frank asked. Sarah had had him back it in there shortly after his struggle with Danny.

"Sure, the police will find it there well after you and I are gone on to our new life together. We'll drive your brother's Prius back to Pittsburgh. You can return it to him, and we'll take my Mercedes to the airport, then off to Samoa."

"You have our reservations and tickets?"

"Of course," Sarah replied, reaching over to her purse on the island and pulling out the ticket folder. She did not, however, hand it to Frank or take the one ticket for herself out of the folder. "Right here, ready to go."

They served the pizza, took their plates over to the breakfast table in the small bay window at the end of the kitchen, overlooking the bay. They sat to enjoy what was intended to be Frank's last meal. If Danny had not been so sick with his pounding head and debilitating cramps, the way they nuzzled and cooed like lovesick teenagers while munching on slices of pizza would have just about sickened him. Sarah's acting ability should have put her on the stage or even qualified her for movie stardom, but she would have said that she had sacrificed any dreams of her own to be the adoring and supportive minister's wife, a role that she really believed had been forced on her.

Instead of struggling to free himself somehow, Danny genuinely struggled to stay conscious and hang onto his faith and hope. He was feeling truly helpless.

CHAPTER FORTY-ONE

It was close to 11:00 Sunday night when Sarah came downstairs and told Frank that it was time. Danny was semi-conscious, hurting like hell, cramped beyond belief, but instantly alert at her words. He decided that it was better if he continued to act only partially conscious at best, so he moaned and dropped his head while Frank cut the tape around his ankles, freeing them from the chair legs. Frank seemed to enjoy pushing him over face-first, producing an even louder moan from Danny. Frank then slid the back of the chair roughly out of the rope wrapped around Danny's chest.

Frank wrestled him up and plunked him down hard on the same chair, wrists still taped behind him and the tape still over his mouth.

"He's going to be very wobbly when I pull him up to his feet," Frank said to Sarah. "You'd better grab the other arm so that we can walk him down to the boat house."

Danny continued to act woozy and ready to fall down as Sarah put an arm under his left, while Frank held him up on the right. In truth, falling down was about the only thing he felt as though he could do, but he hoped that improved circulation in the next few minutes would restore some strength and balance to his legs after so many hours of being bound to the chair.

He kept his eyes shut and continued to groan a bit as the two of them struggled to walk him out of the house, down the sloping path to the boat house toward the door to his final means of transportation. Danny prayed and willed for the ability to run before they got him there. Sarah, in charge and determined as always, ordered Frank again.

"When we get him inside, hold on to him while I start the motor. Then I'll come back to the dock and we can push him in together."

Frank nodded in agreement, having no idea that while he held Danny, Sarah would not only start the motor idling, but also pull the drain plug, letting water seep into the boat. Her wet suit was already stored on board.

Danny remembered that just before they would reach the boat house there was a path leading to the north toward the neighbors' lake cottage. He continued to stagger weakly with the two of them holding him up under each arm until they reached the pitch-black path. The woods it led into were even darker as Sarah had left all lights down toward the bay turned off.

With a sharp pull that he wasn't sure he was capable of, he jerked his right arm out of Frank's grasp and lunged toward that side with enough power to knock Frank off his feet. In the same motion, he jerked with his left arm and spun Sarah around so that she staggered off-balance against the boat house door.

Rid of both of them for an instant, Danny took off and ran for all his worth down the gravelly path into the dark night.

"For God's sake, catch him," Sarah shouted to Frank as she picked herself up, but Frank had already regained his feet and run after Danny.

It was clumsy for Danny to try to run with his arms and wrists bound behind his back, and the tape on his mouth restricted his breathing, but he ran as hard as he could. If he had had more of a head start, he would have looked for a place to hide, try to rub through the infernal tape on a sharp rock, and look for a lake house where somebody was staying that spring. All he could do was run as fast as possible.

It wasn't fast enough under the circumstances. Maybe fifty yards down the path Frank caught up to him and took him down with a hard tackle. Danny squirmed and tried to kick Frank off of him, but he was firmly pinned. Sarah arrived to help regain control of their captive. Frank reached back with clenched fist to smash Danny in the face again, but Sarah caught his wrist.

"Don't bother, sweetheart," she commanded. "We have him, and we don't have time for you to continue the fight. Besides, if you knock him out again, he'll be completely dead weight to have to carry back there."

Danny was more concerned that now he would end up completely dead. The two of them grabbed him as before, hoisted him up, and forcibly walked him with minimal struggle back to the Brand boat house.

CHAPTER FORTY-TWO

As the three reached the boathouse door, Frank shifted behind Danny and grabbed both of his arms. Sarah opened the door. With more desperation and fear than chance of success, Danny revived his struggle by bracing his right foot against the door frame and pushing back against Frank. He tried to snap his still-aching head back to strike Frank's chin. Frank lifted Danny partially off the ground and forced him into the boathouse, feet flailing. Sarah, still holding the door open, hissed at Frank with exasperation.

"Come on, get him in here."

"I'm trying," Frank barked back, sounding exasperated. He whispered sharply into Danny's ear, "A man should know and accept when he's lost."

The brief stalemate at the door was unexpectedly interrupted by a bright light from the direction of the Brand summer home. None of them had heard a car pull into the driveway, then drive out onto the lawn, its headlights shining down across the backyard on the boat house. The three of them paused at the open boat house door, pivoted, and stared up at the headlights.

As they stood virtually frozen in their tracks, a huge silhouette exploded around the car and came hurtling down the slope toward them. A powerful voice boomed out.

"Stop right there, you bastards."

Sarah and Danny knew instantly that it was Tiny.

Frank was momentarily paralyzed. He still held Danny's arms, but swiveled his head desperately. His gaze traveled from one possible hiding spot to another.

Sarah reached clumsily into her windbreaker jacket, trying to extract the snub-nosed .38 revolver. But her hand fumbled with the handle and trigger guard as the little handgun caught in the pocket.

As he reached Danny and Sarah, Tiny saw that she was trying to extract the gun. He leveled her with one swing of his big fist, and the .38 fell to the ground.

Frank ran in the direction of the Prius parked in the drive outside the house. He was halfway across the lawn when another large figure hurtled out of the bright light bathing the yard and took him down like a defensive end sacking a quarterback running for his life. Frank didn't even start to fight back as a crushing knee on his back pinned him to the ground, while a powerful hand smashed his head into the grass and dirt.

Slick growled, "A man should know and accept when he's lost."

Back at the boathouse door, Sarah was down for the count, out cold. Tiny kicked the gun away and reached down to help Danny to his unsteady feet while also removing the tape from his mouth. Danny was once more almost speechless, stammering and trying to find words.

"Tiny...why are you...how did you...find me?"

"Hey man," Tiny replied with his typical roar, "I promised you protection services, and I deliver. Just put a little drama into it so that you would appreciate me more." And he laughed as usual at his own joke.

"Here," he continued, "turn around and I'll get you free."

He pulled out a big switchblade that he still carried from his street gang days – because street hood in baggy pants or business man in an expensive suit, he never went anywhere without his knife. Carefully slicing through the duct tape, he enabled Danny to bring his arms around in front of himself for the first time in many hours. They felt so cramped and painful that

Danny didn't think he could use them just yet.

Tiny turned back to Sarah, lifted her limp body up onto his shoulder like a big burlap bag of potatoes, and turned to go up to the house. His boy Slick, meanwhile, had Frank under control, shaking with fear that Slick might do what he threatened and slice off private parts if he so much as flinched.

But before the five of them could make it back to the house, flashing lights and sirens coming down Stony Point Road announced the arrival of sheriff deputies, who pulled into the Brand driveway as the five reached it. The deputies jumped out right away, drawing their guns.

The chief deputy shouted, "Hold it right there, don't move, arms up, hands where I can see them."

Tiny, Slick, Frank, and Danny to the best of his ability, all complied. Sarah lay crumpled where she had been dropped, like a sack of potatoes.

CHAPTER FORTY-THREE

Danny tried to the best of his woozy ability to explain to the deputies what had been going on just then, but the chief deputy said that it was too much to sort out on the scene. The two African-Americans were handcuffed and put into patrol cars, as was Frank Lewis, who seemed eager to be under protective custody.

A quick check with flashlights and direct questions indicated that Danny was suffering from concussion symptoms, and Sarah was feebly trying to regain her own consciousness as she was helped to get up and sit down in another patrol car. The .38 revolver and the switchblade were at least temporarily confiscated.

At the chief's direction, one of the deputies had called for Fire and Rescue help, and in a matter of minutes two ambulances joined the scene from nearby Suttons Bay. For a small North Woods town, the medical and emergency services were first-rate and quick to respond.

Danny and Sarah were both placed on gurneys with head support and taken to the emergency room of Munson Medical Center in Traverse City, just 20 minutes back down Highway 22 by ambulance. Once there, physicians checked both of them out in separate bays, each one accompanied by a Leelanau County deputy to make sure neither was going anywhere.

Tiny, Slick, and Frank were each taken to the Leelanau County Administrative Center on Highway 204, the campus of which included the Sheriff's Department and county lock-up.

Frank protested loudly, "Keep me away from those two," as he indicated the two Pittsburgh Hill District residents. and the night desk sergeant decided that based on what initial reports were coming into him, it would be a good idea to separate the three from each other in holding cells.

The sergeant was absolutely certain that the two African-American men from Pittsburgh were the ones already wanted for having fled from a deputy after being pulled over for driving 20 miles over the posted speed limit near the border with Grand Traverse County to the south. The Caucasian fellow was protesting that he was a prominent Episcopal priest who was being detained for no reason, but he was dressed more like a wannabe lumberjack and had obviously been in an altercation that left him visibly bruised and smeared with dirt and grass stains. It was probably not a coincidence that the professed priest was also a resident of Pittsburgh, as learned from his driver's license.

"Yup," the sergeant mumbled to himself, "it's gonna take a while to sort this out."

Checks on all three men's driver's licenses showed no outstanding warrants anywhere. The two African-Americans had actually been the most cooperative – no resistance to arrest, respect shown to the deputies on the scene at the Brand summer home, and complete compliance with what they were told to do. The sergeant smiled to himself and indulged in a private speculation that the two were thoroughly familiar with the drill.

The alleged priest, however, had been noisy, trying to jerk away when being led into a cell occupied by a couple of local patrons of a late-closing bar in Lake Leelanau who were sleeping off their previously-rowdy drunkenness. Over his protests demanding badge numbers, Frank was pushed in and locked up while the whole matter was investigated further. If necessary in order to hold him, he would be at least charged with resisting arrest and assaulting a police officer.

Both Danny and Sarah were admitted to rooms in the hospital for scans, further examination, and observation – their respective deputies posting outside their assigned rooms. Having determined that both of them were stable and capable of being questioned, a sheriff detective interviewed each of them separately. It was immediately evident that Danny showed signs of having been held captive, and his story checked out about having been assaulted in the Brand home and held against his will by Sarah and Frank, who had planned his murder.

Sarah, meanwhile, had been gathering her thoughts as her head cleared, and she desperately tried to pass off the story that both Danny and she had been subdued and held captive by Frank, who had followed them from Pittsburgh in the green Prius after having murdered her husband a week ago. Her previous mastery of details and meticulous planning failed in her spontaneous concoction, however, and she didn't think of the fact that she had not gotten to the point of faking the duct tape on her wrists and ankles, nor the bump and bruise she had intended to inflict upon herself to fake an assault by Frank.

It had also been quickly determined at the Leelanau County Sheriff's Department that the .38 snub-nose was registered to her husband, William Brand, and that she had been in possession of it at the scene at the Brand's summer home. Her prints were the only ones on the weapon, and it checked out that she had stowed it in her jacket pocket, without a concealed carry permit. Details started to pull together that she was a perpetrator, not a victim as she claimed. It also didn't help her case that a detective's sweep of the Brand house on Stony Point immediately found luggage clustered together in the upstairs hall tagged as belonging to her and to Frank, respectively.

While circumstantial, the suitcases suggested that the two had planned to leave together, and further time and investigation would disclose fingerprints of the two all over the bedroom, as well as bodily fluid evidence on the sheets of the bed. Danny's prints were nowhere to be found in the upper level of the house. It didn't take long to determine that his entire account of what happened there was nothing but the truth.

By later that Monday morning the deputy was pulled off of his room, while direct orders were given to the deputy watching Sarah that as soon as she was medically cleared to be discharged, another deputy would join him and take her directly to the women's section of the county jail to await further investigation and charges.

This affair would require a lot more attention on the part of police and sheriff departments in both Pennsylvania and Michigan. It had all the makings of a pretty spectacular collar for the sheriff's deputies, and not bad for the sheriff himself, either.

The two African-American men checked out as well. The only crime they were responsible for was driving over the posted speed limit and fleeing when stopped by a patrol car. They were ticketed, instructed on what they had to do to settle the citation, and commended for their part in stopping the abduction in process, and very likely an intended murder.

They were released that Monday morning and wished a good trip back to Pennsylvania. They deserved credit, but that didn't mean the two tough-looking fellows needed to stay in usually peaceful Leelanau. The switchblade was kept as possible evidence, but it would make a neat souvenir in the desk sergeant's private collection eventually. Not a bad night's work for their little department...and a much better story than throwing two drunks into the holding cell to sleep it off.

CHAPTER FORTY-FOUR

Monday afternoon after the hospital food service served Danny lunch in his room, Tiny and Slick came in wearing visitor badges. They had grabbed a couple of huge sandwiches for themselves at the 45th Parallel Café in Suttons Bay after being released from the Leelanau County lock-up, and then had driven down to Munson Hospital to see Danny. The room was standard size for a hospital, but with the machines hooked up to him, the chair, the bed tray, and the startled nurse who was checking him just then, the two giant men who came in seemed to stuff the room to the maximum.

The two nodded politely to the nurse, who went off to check on her other patients, and Tiny boomed out loud enough to drown out the intercom, "There he is, goofing off while we do all the work."

Slick added, "Dr. Henriks, you feeling okay now?"

"Much better, guys. Come over here. Both last night and today, you're a sight for sore eyes," Danny answered. Tiny and Slick bent over to hug him in turn.

"Man, we were worried about you, Danny," Tiny said with great sincerity. "And it turns out, for good reason."

"Sit down, guys. Start from the beginning and tell me how you got up here and found me."

"Slick, go get yourself a chair," Tiny ordered as he sat down in the one at Danny's bedside.

Slick went out to the nurses' station and politely asked if he could borrow another chair. The charge nurse, who wasn't intimidated by doctors, administrators, or anyone from the inner city of Pittsburgh, pointed down the hall a short way and said, "You can use that one, but you better put it back when you leave."

"Yes'm," Slick agreed. The woman was used to being obeyed. He returned with his assigned chair and sat on the other side of Danny's bed.

"Well, it all started when we conducted our first protection service on Dr. Brand's house, like you asked," Tiny began their story. "Saturday afternoon after you and Mrs. Brand left to drive up here, Slick, Speed, and I drove over to Shadyside and checked it out. House was shut up tight, no signs that anyone was messing around, no little green car around, everything cool."

"Yah," Slick joined in. "But then we went around to the garage, and I saw the filled-up garbage can."

"Garbage can?" Danny wondered. Tiny shot a glance at Slick that conveyed *don't interrupt me, fool,* but Slick went on in his enthusiasm.

"Garbage can," he confirmed, nodding his head. "Mrs. Brand had it filled up, but with no room left, there was this big, flat, bakery box left right on top, on the lid. I was driving Tiny's Lincoln, and I stopped, got out, and looked in the box. It was over half full of donuts, man, big ones, too."

"Yes," Danny confirmed, "the ladies of the church had brought over so much food to the rectory, the family and I just couldn't eat it all, so since we were leaving, Sarah took the leftovers out early Saturday morning and put them there before I arrived."

"So," Tiny added, "Slick and Speed and I made use of the donuts – wouldn't be right to let them go to waste....unless it was our waists." Tiny laughed at himself.

"Then," he continued, "we went back there about lunchtime on Sunday, yesterday; we did our same check. All good and quiet. Then we swung back around to the garage. The garbage can was still there, full, hadn't been collected yet, of course, and Slick here decides that he needs to get out and actually look inside it. I think he was hoping he had missed more donuts the first stop, plus he was getting hungry."

"Well, I thought there be no harm in looking," Slick admitted. "And there was lots of food dumped in there – all mushed up, but I also spotted an airline itinerary sheet, kind of crumpled up, and I just got curious about who was going where."

Tiny took over the story again. "So he brings the paper over to me in the car, and shows it to me. I read it over, and it shows a reservation for a Mrs. Sarah Brand, departing Pittsburgh International Tuesday morning on United Airlines, final destination, Samoa."

"Yah, Samoa," Slick agreed, reluctant to give over his part of the story, but Tiny pushed on with determination.

"So I gets to thinking about that. You had made it very definite that you and Mrs. Brand were going back to Pittsburgh, leaving here this morning, and that once the two of you were back there, that she had lots of post-funeral stuff to do, going through Dr. Brand's clothes, all that. So why would she have a plane reservation to Samoa on Tuesday?"

"It turned out," Danny explained, "that once she was rid of me, and then set up her lover Frank to drown out in the big bay, she was going to drive right back to Shadyside in that green Prius, gather up what she needed, and fly one-way to Samoa the next day to spend the rest of her days in untouchable luxury."

"Samoa," Tiny nodded, "no extradition treaty with the U.S." Tiny knew such things.

"Turns out that she was planning to become a serial killer," Danny said. "She went so far as to brag to me how she had killed her husband Bill with his own shotgun, staging it to look like a suicide, almost got away with it, but then I kept poking around. Not only was there a curious little detail about the gun, but I also refused to believe that Bill would have any reason to take his own life."

"You know," Tiny got excited, "they always say, look first at the spouse if there's a suspicious death. And with you looking into how Dr. Brand died, then Slick finding that crumpled-up itinerary, I'm going over that in my head. Why would she lie about being there in Pittsburgh when she was actually planning to fly one-way to Samoa? So I'm thinking as we were driving back to the Hill, what if she actually murdered him, and what if she lured you up here to their summer home to get rid of you and your meddling?"

"Which is precisely what she did and had planned, with dumb Frank's help," Danny confirmed again. "So, what did you do then?"

"Well, I first tried to call you on your cell, to at least tell you what we found. That itinerary she didn't need anymore and thought she was throwing away, and warn you about my suspicions. But you didn't answer, went right to voicemail."

"Oh, that's right," the light went on in Danny's still-dulled mind. "When I left the Brand lake home Sunday morning to go over to the Cedar Rod & Gun Club, I realized that I had left my cell phone at the bed and breakfast I stayed at Saturday night. I told Sarah that she could try to reach me at the gun range if she needed to call. Then when I got back to the Brand's place, that was when Frank jumped me, I got bound to a chair, and I never had a chance to go back to get my phone. It's still sitting there. The lady at the bed and breakfast must wonder what happened to me that I didn't stay there last night."

"Not as much as we wondered what was happening to you," Tiny said.

"Yah," Slick agreed. "When you didn't answer your cell, we were afraid that she had already whacked you."

Tiny went on, "I thought about calling the police, the sheriff, up here to go check on you, but we didn't really have anything to go on but suspicions and hearsay."

"Besides," Slick jumped in again, "why would they listen to a couple of black brothers way over there in Pittsburgh?" Tiny ignored him and continued.

"So all I could think of to do was drive up here ourselves. I left Speed to take care of things back in the Hill; Slick and I grabbed a couple of duffels for ourselves. We always keep them packed and ready, you know, in case we get a sudden-like urge to take a vacation break from our business on the Hill. And, we hit the road."

"Yah," Slick smiled. "Made it to Leelanau County in about

eight hours. Dodged those state trooper speed traps every time."

"Honesty compels, though," Tiny admitted. "We wouldn't have cut it so close in saving your sorry ass, 'cept for the Rehnquist ruling."

"The Rehnquist ruling?" Danny was mystified.

"Yah, old Chief Justice Rehnquist. You remember him. Well, some years back a couple of Southern California dudes," Tiny explained, "made a business trip to Milwaukee in January. They were stopped by a police car; the officers searched and found quite a stash of drugs. They were arrested on the spot. The defense made the case that it was an illegal stop and search and seizure. Which it was. They hadn't been doing anything to cause the stop and arrest. Made it all the way to the Supreme Court, and old chief justice Bill wrote the opinion upholding the arrest and conviction. Said that there was reasonable justification on the part of the police, 'cause what else would two Latino cats with California plates be doing in Milwaukee in January?"

"And that pertained to you two how?"

"Well duh," Tiny chided him, "Here we had two black brothers from Pennsylvania with angry demeanor hustling up Highway 22 into Leelanau, sporting gold chains and driving a big, black Lincoln. Do we look like a couple of spring vacationers from somewhere down south of Michigan? Clearly not, so this sheriff car pulls us over at one of the roadside picnic areas."

"You forgot the part where we were doing 65-70 in that 40 mph zone," Slick pointed out.

"No matter," Tiny waved him off. "We were on a mission; didn't know why Danny here wasn't answering his phone, what might have happened to him, what that Brand lady was up to. We didn't have time to sit for some license check and writing no citation."

"So when the deputy went back to his car to run your plates, you just took off," Danny concluded.

"Better believe it. Weren't no way we were going to sell him the story that we were up here all the way from Pittsburgh on a rescue mission. Figured the best way to get the authorities to the Brand place was to force them to chase us."

"And it worked," Slick beamed.

"I'm sure glad it did," Danny said with a big smile and sigh of relief. "And it all started because yesterday morning Slick here was hoping for some more donuts."

Shrugging with a little embarrassment, Slick protested, "Hey, I was hungry. And those Saturday donuts were gooood!"

All three of them roared with laughter, even if it made Danny's head hurt some more. Finally settling down, Tiny asked Danny, "So when does the doc say you can get out of here?"

"If everything looks okay," Danny answered, "he promised to sign my release tomorrow morning. I was supposed to be back at my church in Pittsburgh by then, but I'll call the office this afternoon and let Mildred know not to expect me until Wednesday. And I'll have to go back to the Brand house and retrieve my Jeep to drive back."

"No worries, Dr. Henriks," Slick assured him. "Give me the keys and I'll go up this afternoon and get it for you. I'd go to that bed and breakfast and collect your stuff there, too, but your lady hostess might not be comfortable with that. In fact, I'll drive you up there tomorrow morning; we can get your things, and then Tiny and I will take turns driving you and your Grand Cherokee all the way back to Pittsburgh. Won't we, Tiny?"

Tiny laughed so loud as to make heads look up out at the nurses' station, "You bet your sweet ass we will. After all, I run a complete protection service, even with home delivery." All three of them roared, and the head nurse herself came over to settle things down.

CHAPTER FORTY-FIVE

It had been another long drive from Leelanau County, Michigan, to Pittsburgh, but with Slick and Tiny taking turns driving Danny's Jeep for him, he was able to put the seat back and catch cat naps along the way. Back at his South Hills home around 9:00 Tuesday night, Danny, Tiny and Slick shook hands and hugged before the two drove back to the Hill. They got in their car and Danny leaned over and spoke to them through the Lincoln's front window.

"Again, guys, I can't thank you enough. I was a goner unless you showed up the way you did. Tiny, your protection services are the greatest. For me, at least. And, Slick, I owe you a big box of donuts, man."

Tiny answered from the passenger's side, "Aw, it was fun, Danny. I never got to hit a woman before. And she certainly had it coming. You get some rest, brother, and schedule that follow-up with your doctor tomorrow morning, you hear?"

"I will," Danny assured him. "And I'll never forget what you did for me, driving all that way up there to save my ass."

"That's what friends are for," Tiny replied, holding up his wrist with that faded, old friendship bracelet still on. And off they drove.

With the rest on the drive back and the release of a lot of tension, Danny felt drained but amazingly relaxed. Before turning in for the night, he decided to pour himself some of his Crown Royal Black and head out to the patio and his favorite Adirondack chair. He slipped a jacket on to ward off the chill of the spring night.

It was nothing like the normally peaceful Leelanau with its woods and water, but a relatively quiet evening for the Pittsburgh area, just a couple of jet airliners overhead going to and from Pittsburgh International. He couldn't help but mentally list the obvious losses and gains from Easter Sunday to the Sunday following.

Lost was Bill Brand, probably his best friend, murdered in his own church study by a wife who resented beyond belief his attention to everything besides her, including that church organist. Will Congreve got it right: hell hath no fury like that of a woman scorned.

Lost was certainly his longest-friend and former lover, Sarah Brand. Compounding the tragedy of the last ten days was the now-obvious fact that Sarah had been fatally flawed for many years, consumed by bitterness and resentment toward Bill that she had hidden from virtually everyone. It would take months, if not a year or more, for the extent of her crimes to be investigated fully, brought to trial, conviction and sentencing obtained. Who knows how many years of incarceration ahead of her, possibly her remaining life span.

Lost was an almost two thousand year-old fragment of papyrus that surely would have contributed to many people's understandings and beliefs about the most influential man who has ever lived on earth. Despite many who would have rejected what it had to say, the first-century text would have added more to the story of the man Jesus, whom they came to call the Christ.

Lost was a talented young Episcopal priest who had been privileged to serve in such a prestigious church and learn from such a prominent rector and pastor. Frank Lewis possessed his own flaws that proved fatal to him. He was consumed by jealousy and envy, resented being in a subordinate position, and was gullible and lustful enough to believe that the extremely wealthy and lovely wife of his boss would want to love him and run away with him to a South Pacific island. He, too, would be going away for a long time once convicted and sentenced.

Danny was feeling a bit gloomy about his list of losses, including probably being a measure of his own naivete about people whom he assumed were friends but proved not to be...to a murderous extreme. He took a good, strong sip of the whiskey and decided he needed to turn to a more positive side of his personal ledger. What was gained?

Gained was certainly some degree of revelation and truth. The kind of people Sarah and Frank truly were had been brought into the light for all to see. In addition to Danny, there were scholars, researchers, and technicians who had seen and studied the papyrus. They knew what it said and what it could contribute to Christian understanding of the Lord Jesus. Photos had been taken, statements and reports written; the discussion and debate would go on. And yes, the original fragment had been destroyed and lost, but there was always a chance, however slight, that some other piece testifying to the same contention could be found.

Gained also was perhaps some increased confidence in his own feelings and instincts. However compulsive Daniel Henriks could be in many aspects of his life and work, he knew that had he not continued to reject the idea that his friend Bill would ever commit suicide, and had he not obsessed over the little detail of the shotgun choke tube, Bill's murder in the church might not have been revealed and Sarah might have gotten away with it.

But undoubtedly the biggest gain, Danny nodded to himself, was the confirmation of the fact that he really did have true friends. Had not Tiny and his "boys," Slick and Speed gone many extra miles for him, Sarah would have ended up with three murders in her tally. Yet again, events had proven that genuine friendship lies not in words, but in the actions that confirm them.

Friends, Danny smiled, are those people who really are there for you when the going gets tough...and especially when your life hangs in the balance. James, the brother of Jesus, had that one right in the New Testament book bearing his name. Faith, and mere words, without deeds are dead. And dead he would have been had it not been for his friends. Their last-minute rescue had been next-to-impossible.

Danny took another sip of the Crown Royal Black. It tasted even better, and life was indeed good. It certainly beat the alternative.

* * *

Had Danny been able to look behind him on his patio and see what was invisible to his physical sight, he would have beheld a figure in dazzling clothes standing behind and over him. The presence was a pure spiritual being, almost always existing in a spectrum of light, energy and divine power beyond human ability to see, measure, or detect in any way. Its existence and presence was rarely perceived unless there was a divine reason to reveal to human senses, and then usually only by an inner, spiritual feeling rather than in physical forms.

Danny's rescue seemed virtually impossible to him before and when it occurred, but with God, and God's heavenly beings, nothing is impossible. During all that had happened to him, for this moment, and for a long time to come, the Angel of Providence and Protection would stand guard over him, accompany him, and support him through the peaks and valleys of the journey of his life. Danny need not fear even the valley of the shadow of death. And in God's good time, one day he would pass over to rejoin all those who had gone on before him...including his best friend, Bill.

The End

If you liked this book, you will be pleased to know that the second book in the *Death Most Unholy* series is currently being prepared for publication.

Here is an excerpt of:

Death Crashes the Wedding

Still in his black pulpit robe with its three velvet stripes on each billowing sleeve and a white, gold-embroidered, fringed stole around his neck and draped down the front of the robe, the Rev. Dr. Daniel Henriks descended the main steps outside the church.

He joined Mark, Tim, Tiny and Angela as they clustered on the walk, hugging and rejoicing after the beautiful wedding.

The Angel of Death sped unseen up the front walk in the opposite direction, matching the velocity of the approaching bullet. The .308, 168-grain, boat-tailed bullet ripped through the voluminous sleeve of Danny's right arm from the back as he put his arm around Angela. It struck her in the back of her upper torso and tore through soft flesh to hit Mark standing in front of them, smiling at their congratulations.

The Angel invisibly gathered the exiting soul in what would have seemed like a great vessel scooping up a lone drop as it fell from the body, if it were possible to ascribe bodily form to a purely spiritual event. The Angel and the soul swept instantly into the timelessness of Eternity, into the spiritual Kingdom of Heaven, before the dead shell of the victim had even struck the concrete below it.

ABOUT THE AUTHOR

 The Rev. Dr. David Quincy Hall is a retired Presbyterian pastor living with his beloved wife, the Rev. Maxine, their daughter, and their English Springer Spaniel, Ember. At the writing of *Death Comes to the Rector* they resided in scenic Leelanau County, Michigan.

David is a lifelong outdoors man who still enjoys fly fishing for trout and upland bird hunting with Ember in the streams and forests he loves so much. Upon retiring from parish ministry he published a number of magazine articles about aspects of those outdoor sports. In more recent years he turned to writing mystery novels, of which *Death Comes to the Rector* is only the first.

During his professional career, David served congregations across the country in Pennsylvania, Michigan, Iowa, Wisconsin and California, and in diverse settings including metropolitan, inner city, medium-sized and small cities, small town, rural, suburban and the North Woods. Firsthand experience living in those different areas provides rich and accurate details for the scenes and settings in his books. Even more, his greatly diverse experience with all kinds of people in his work helps to create characters who are authentic and believable as you meet them.

Death Comes to the Rector is the first book of the *Death Most Unholy* series.

Printed in Great Britain
by Amazon